The
Message

A novel by
Yan Vana

Falcondale Press

ASIN: B019NDIP1A
ISBN: 978-1527204966

INTRODUCTION

The Message by Yan Vana is a surprisingly comprehensive overview of the environmental problems caused by over population. It brings most of the available knowledge together in one place but does so in a readable way. What makes it unique is that, unlike most other works on the environment, it is written not from man's point of view, but from that of the other occupants of our planet.

The book follows an official inquiry into the wanton destruction of a protected nature reserve. The first witnesses give evidence of the extent of the damage and later witnesses identify those responsible. As the plot unfolds it becomes apparent that the nature reserve is Earth and that the inquiry is being undertaken by regulators from other galaxies who have responsibility for the protection of nature reserves throughout the cosmos.

Over the years Authors have used fiction to draw attention to social or political issues we would all prefer to ignore. Examples would be Oliver Twist, Uncle Tom's Cabin, Hard Times, The Grapes of Wrath, To Kill a Mockingbird and Animal Farm.

It is tempting to compare *The Message* with George Orwell's Animal Farm in that in both, the characters are not human. However whilst Animal Farm can be defined as allegorical, The Message although being, on the face

2

of it, fantasy or science fiction is in fact telling a straight forward factual message.

The use of fantasy or science fiction in *The Message* is simply there to make an otherwise unwelcome message palatable. Whether they agree with it or not the message it is conveying will be clear to any reader without the need for explanation. In many ways it can be said to combine some of the allegorical format of Orwell's Animal Farm with his grim factual reporting in A Road to Wigan Pier and the dystopian nature of his 1984.

Underneath the science fiction and fantasy *The Message* is a serious philosophical study of the relationship between man and the rest of nature. It questions many preconceived beliefs; in particular that technological advancement is a sign of superiority rather than simply an acceptance that, from an evolutionary standpoint, man is physically backward and has to rely on tools to do things which other species, we regard as inferior, can do naturally.

That is not to say that the plot is merely a platform for an undisguised moral message. To many it will also be a sad and moving love story, to others a study of humanity and for others a perceptive view of twenty first century Environmental Regulation.

Concern as to overpopulation is nothing new. Thomas Malthus's 'An Essay on the Principle of Population' was first published in 1798 and went on to five further editions over the next thirty years. Despite his name, Malthus was a rural English Clergyman. The publication of The Message coincides with the 250th Anniversary of his birth.

Although there have been a number of other, mainly scholarly, works on overpopulation since then the most significant recent contribution is probably 'The Population Bomb' by Professor Paul Ehrlich (1968). This attracted heavy criticism for its, as it transpired, inaccurate prediction that hundreds of millions would die in the 1970's and 80's through starvation as a result of overpopulation. The fact is that when Ehrlich wrote 'The Population Bomb' in 1968 the human population was still under four billion and has nearly doubled since then.

However it is arguable that Ehrlich's prediction only proved wrong because he underestimated the extent man could and would go to provide not just the extra food but also all the other things necessary to support an ever increasing population. This has been achieved by clearing more and more wild and forested areas, (particularly the rain forest) for intensive agriculture; the wanton use of pesticides, artificial fertilisers and genetic engineering; and the plundering and industrialisation of the Planet. 'The Message' is that it is the resulting damage to the Earth which is now the real threat to man.

Some may think that if we had listened to Ehrlich in the early 1970's, rather than rejecting his warnings just because his immediate predictions were wrong, there would still have been time to take the necessary actions. Now fifty years on there is a real risk we may have left it too late.

It could be said that Malthus was warning what could happen. Ehrlich was predicting what was about to happen and Vana is telling us what is happening.

Although there have been a number of individuals and organisations campaigning on the subject of overpopulation over the years these have mainly been academic intellectuals. There has been no populist campaigner, such as a William Wilberforce, Emmeline Pankhurst, Gandhi, Martin Luther King or Nelson Mandela, who are prepared to put up with the inevitable personal vilification and rebuffs to get up and shout the message, and keep on shouting it, until people start to listen. It is Yan Vana's hope that this book will help to rekindle the debate and encourage everyone concerned to get up and start putting the message across.

The Message was Vana's original choice as the title. Halfway through editing he changed it to *The Inquiry* thinking that was more descriptive of the plot. He was eventually persuaded by his wife to go back to *The Message* which she considered to better convey the purpose of the book.

The original idea for *The Message* came to the Author in 2010. He sketched out the first chapter in 2013 but did not return to it until August 2014 when he then completed the first draft from beginning to end in ten weeks. After a year of editing and revision *The Message* was finally published worldwide on Amazon Kindle in December 2015.

Friends of Retha   February 2016

THE END

They left early this morning.
I saw them slowly fade into the distance.
They were so close together it was as if they were one.
Then they were gone.

THE
MESSAGE

Private Journal

The message was waiting for me when I got back from seeing Setar. It had been a difficult meeting. I suppose it was my fault not to have realised she would take it so badly, I should have given her at least some warning. We have been very close and her response was touching. Retirement is one of those things we talk about but I am not sure many of us really plan for it. I certainly didn't.

It just became obvious to me one day that it was time to go. I am not sure there was anything in particular that provoked it. It could have been that I was just becoming tired of it all, but I am not sure it was that. It certainly wasn't my health, that is still surprisingly good allowing for my age.

No, I just think I realised that the time had come. That everyone was ready for a change. That I had nothing more to add. I suppose it has been an enormous responsibility but I am not sure I ever felt it. I always thought myself privileged to be called upon and I have never had any regrets.

I have been fortunate to have been here at a time when we have been able to make real progress. I haven't felt held back by the jealousies and in-fighting of the past. Some have been kind enough to attribute this to me. I do not know whether that is true but if it is it is more reason to go whilst that is what I might be remembered for.

I hope I said the right things. I had to promise a longer hand over than I had intended.

The message was lying on my desk with a note on it saying "I think this was meant for you. I am sorry we opened it." It was an old fashioned message pad of the kind we used a long time ago. No-one has called me Mitzo for ages. I only used it for a very short time when I was in training. It helped to give me a bit of anonymity which made things easier.

My first reaction was surprise that there was anyone still alive who would remember me by that name. When you get to my age there are few acquaintances of youth remaining. I looked for the name at the bottom. "Avsa"

Suddenly I was back in Retha all that time ago. Memories long forgotten, some good, some painful started to flood back. Some things I had deliberately not thought of for half a life time.

We were above this stunning waterfall. The sound of the water thundering down into the river below. Trees covered all the land around in a profusion of bright green vegetation. Birds flew across the tree tops. A kaleidoscope of bright colours dropping in and out of the trees. Much larger hunting birds with dark colouring and intimidating beaks hovering a bit above waiting for the opportunity to swoop.

The occasional sound of animals moving on the forest floor. The glimpse of creatures of some kind just under the surface of the river. But nothing else. Just the two of us and that unspoilt paradise.

It was our first day. I had no idea what trees or birds or animals I was seeing or hearing. Avsa would point them out but there was too much to take in. I could have stayed watching for ever but the short days, which I never got used to, meant that we could only catch tiny glimpses of each area.

From there Avsa took us further inland to a high country of dry brown plains with enormous mountains in the distance. At first there seemed little there, but as I concentrated I realised I was looking at vast herds of animals. Some horned. Some small and agile. All amazingly wonderful, some more than others. One with yellowy tan splotches and enormous long legs and neck. Another grey, leathery and gigantic with long nose and ears.

All moving in an unspoilt habitat they had lived in long before we came. All totally unconcerned by us.

The occasional reed edged lake was home to vast flocks of wild fowl. White and black and pink and yellow and a mixture of all four. Rising and falling in groups above the water. Landing and feeding, then for no apparent reason taking off in a vast cloud and swirling around, until whatever had disturbed them was gone or forgotten, and then landing back onto the water.

The movement of all those flocks of birds and herds of animals was continuous as if orchestrated as a ballet. You didn't need to know what they all were or why they were there or where they were going to or coming from. The spectacle was enough.

It was dark before we realised it and it seemed silly to waste all that time going back again just to sleep. We slept on a grass bank under the stars with the sound of the birds and animals all around us. Avsa had been told to show me as much as he could and he took that seriously. The next morning we were up and off as soon as it was light and moving up into the mountains at the back.

At first there was vegetation covering the foothills but it became sparser the higher we got until we moved into an area of rough grass, rock and scree. The odd areas of grassland were filled with brightly coloured flowers with the occasional small animal grazing amongst them. Then we were above even that and into snow and ice going all the way up to the top of the highest mountains with the deep blue sky above. When we were over them the vista fell away from us to an azure sea in the far distance. We slowed, mesmerised by the ice and snow behind and the sea away in the front.

Close to the coast the vegetation changed. The air was different. The trees were not as large. Everything was more colourful. Then almost without warning there were vast expanses of salt lakes and marshes. Whether it was us that disturbed them I do not know but out of nowhere thousands of long legged white birds swarmed in front of us blocking the sky.

I turned to Avsa and said "This is paradise". He smiled and said "That is why we wanted someone like you to see it. This is probably the last totally unspoilt wilderness left anywhere. We must preserve it before it is too late."

I knew that if this had been a major inquiry they wouldn't have chosen me to do it. There were many more experienced career Inspectors to whom it could have been given. I suspected I got it partly because they wanted me to gain experience in the field but also because if I said it was worth preserving, people wouldn't argue. I don't know whether Avsa understood this. I am not sure what he thought or what he knew. I had no sooner got to Retha than the Director had said that Avsa would show me round. I had little time to take it all in let alone get to know him before we started. All I saw was a large rugged slightly embarrassed young warden. Someone who was happier running a reserve than showing a VIP around.

He hardly managed twenty words until we got going and suddenly he was pointing to this and pointing to that. He was using words for the animals and birds we were seeing that meant nothing to me but you couldn't help being lifted by his enthusiasm. His wonder for what was down there.

No one listening to him could be unaffected. A look at something to the left was followed by him pointing out something in the opposite direction. Things I wouldn't have seen without him. I was just mesmerised by the sheer scale and beauty of all we saw. Vast herds of one particular animal followed by another herd of something completely different. A flock of large pink birds suddenly lifting off on one side followed by some totally different birds landing on the other.

The message itself was very short.

MESSAGE

From: Avsa Signe   **To:** HSH
Mitzo *I don't know if you remember me. I was your Guide when you inspected Retha.   Things are very bad there now.   The Directorate asked for an Inquiry by a Council Inspector. That has finished but we haven't heard anything*
Is there anything you can do? ***Avsa***

I was about to go through to Peti to ask her to see if she could find a record of any Inquiry when she walked in. "I thought you might want this, it's the Inquiry Transcript" she said holding a memory file and walked out.

I will miss her.

A few minutes later she came back again. "I am trying to find out why the Inspector's Report isn't available yet. It looks as if the University of Idreji has been trying to stall it. It should have gone through to a Commissioner for a Decision long before now".

"Idreji?" I asked.

"They were given the running of the Reserve some time ago. Retha and a number of other Reserves were taken away from the Conservation Directorate. Budget cuts or something like that. I don't know what Idreji's problem is. It looks as if they are trying to ward off criticism of how they have handled things. They have been raising objections ever since the Inspector's draft Report was circulated."

I lodged the memory file and loaded the Transcript which seemed to take for ever. The Inspector was not one I had heard of before. He was middle ranking and obviously one of the old guard, dependable, but unimaginative. We didn't seem to have treated this as a big issue.

He seemed to have kept competently to the standard format for Inquiries of this kind where the Inspector and most of the witnesses are spread all over the place. He had taken a lot of trouble to help all the interested parties participate all at the same time which is an almost impossible task. With all the communication and technical problems, not to mention the time differences, it takes experience, patience and preparation to ensure things run smoothly.

COUNCIL of COMMISSIONERS
Retha Inquiry Transcript

Inspector.   Welcome to this Inquiry which is being held under Chapter 47 to consider an application to the Council of Commissioners by the Conservation Directorate for a Section 427 Order in respect of the Retha Protected Reserve.

I have been appointed by the Council of Commissioners to carry out this Inquiry and to report my findings to the Commissioners for their decision. As you will all appreciate a Section 427 Order is very rarely applied for and even more rarely granted. The Council therefore must treat such Applications with the utmost seriousness.

It is essential that everyone, who has an interest, has an opportunity to give evidence. As well as posting the necessary Public Notices we have also individually notified all known interested parties. We have now received responses from, I understand, sixteen organisations and individuals. Of those, fourteen have asked to present oral evidence at this hearing and two have submitted recorded submissions.

I imagine that few, if any, of you have attended an Inquiry of this nature before so it might be helpful if I gave a brief explanation of how I intend to conduct it. Because it is not possible to get all the interested parties together in one place at the same time, and because of all the various time differences, an old fashioned inquisitorial Inquiry is not feasible. So in keeping with current practice I will invite each witness giving oral evidence to make a formal statement.   If any of the

13

other parties then has any questions or comments on the evidence being given they should message them to me.

It is important that all those giving oral evidence keep their communicators open for a reasonable time span after they have finished to allow for questions and comments to come in. Equally I would ask anyone who wishes to submit a question or comment to raise it before, or as soon as possible after, that witness has finished their evidence so they can deal with it straight away. I do not want to have to be recalling witnesses and interrupting other evidence.

I intend so far as possible to divide the Inquiry into Three Sections. Firstly any Introductory Submissions. Secondly, evidence on the Issues that have given rise to the request for this Inquiry and Thirdly, the possible Remedies available to the Council. I would ask everyone to ensure that they limit their evidence to that which is relevant to the particular Section we are considering at the time, even if this means dividing their submissions into two parts.

I am anxious to ensure that everyone has the opportunity to give the evidence they wish and to raise comments or questions on the evidence given by others. But I am sure that you all understand that it is equally important that we complete this Inquiry in manageable time scales, so I would ask everyone to be as concise as possible. I understand for example that the Government of the Outuin will wish to address the Inquiry on the question of Remedies but that they will soon be passing out of communication. It is therefore important that they have the opportunity to make their submissions before then if at all possible but I have asked them to submit a recorded copy so that we have that available if it becomes necessary.

By way of explanation, although this is a specific Application for a Section 427 Order, it is open to any of the participants to suggest other remedies and as I say this can be discussed in Section Three. It is of course open to me to decide at the end of Section Two that there is no case to consider in which case we would not then proceed to Section Three.

Although we would like to think it is not essential with this form of Inquiry, it is open to any participants to be legally represented. At the moment only the University of Idreji has notified me that they will be. But if there is anyone else please could you let me know.

Advokate Otto Slaborg. Thank you Inspector. I confirm that I have been instructed by the University of Idreji to represent their interests. As you have already been notified a number of members of the University will be submitting individual evidence but I would wish to make an opening statement in Section One.

Inspector. Thank you Advokate Slaborg.

As I say if anyone else intends to be represented let me know now. If you have not already done so can you ensure that we are notified of your language of choice. Hopefully the technicians will be able to arrange contemporaneous translation for all of you but if anyone finds any difficulties in receiving any of these proceedings please let me know immediately. If you cannot do so via your communicator then please send a message to me – you will all have received my message address. In any event it is shown on the Council's screen.

We will now move to the First Section, of this Application.

Only the Directorate and Advokate Slaborg have given notice that they wish to make opening submissions and I will ask Director Erigh Jonsen of the Conservation Directorate, who is the Applicant, to open first.

Director Erigh Jonsen. Thank you Inspector. Can I first introduce myself. As you have said I am the Director of the Conservation Directorate. We have legal responsibility for all designated Protected Reserves though we do not administer all of them. Retha has been administered by the University of Idreji under contract from the Directorate.

I am very grateful to you and the Council for arranging this Inquiry so promptly particularly in view of all the complexities of communication involved, not only over very large distances but also, I understand, to ten separate jurisdictions.

Retha is a Protected Reserve under Section 365. We do not know exactly when it was first discovered. What I can say is that the Directorate was aware of it and was casting a protective eye over it for a long period before it was formally designated.

Our normal policy is to keep areas like this under scrutiny and only act if it is becoming clear that it is beginning to attract unwelcome attention. You will understand that the actual act of Designation can give a Reserve the very publicity we are trying to avoid. There is also the consideration that protection has very significant cost implications for the Directorate.

There were occasional reports of uninvited visitors, mainly sightseers and some poachers, but nothing that was considered serious enough for Designation. Then quite suddenly, mainly as a result of a report that appeared on an Adventure Programme, there was an explosion of interest and the Directorate was left with no choice. An immediate Interim Supervision Order was issued by the then Director prohibiting all unauthorised visitations of any kind and the Directorate made the formal Application to the Council for Section 365 Protection. That is a time consuming process particularly because of the travel times involved. Even more so then.

An Inspector who was also a Commissioner, which was a bit unusual, was duly appointed to carry out a ground inspection and take evidence from all the staff involved. The Inspection was more lengthy than normal, which I can only assume was as a result of the level of objection received from commercial and tourist interests. The Inspector's subsequent report unequivocally recommended Protected Status which was duly granted by the Council of Commissioners.

The Reserve then passed into the administration of the Directorate's resident Ranger Team. We had in fact already put a team in place as soon as we made the Supervision Order. The Directorate then continued to directly administer the Reserve in the same way as all the rest of its Reserves. Subsequently as a result of budget cutbacks it was decided to put the Administration of Retha and the two other most remote Reserves out to tender. The contract for Retha was ultimately awarded to the University of Idreji, who offered to do it for nothing. They then administered it up to very recently.

The administration of the other two Reserves was given to the Universal Wildlife Protection Fund. I understand they had in fact tendered for all three.

Retha is, in my view, probably the most singular ecological area ever discovered. It's breadth of habitats, landscape, climate, geology and species both botanical and zoological is beyond anything we have ever found elsewhere. It ranges from ice shelfs, to deserts, to rain forests, to mountains, to arid plains and deep seas. Its relatively benign climate and huge areas of ocean combined with its remoteness have enabled species to evolve in greater numbers and variety than anywhere else. The numbers are unbelievable. It is estimated that there could be over ten million different species. That is a figure most of us cannot even imagine.

I have been privileged to visit it but only on one occasion. The distances involved make it virtually impossible to make the journey more than once in a lifetime. It is quite simply awesomely beautiful. I have never seen anything to compare with it and I have had the good fortune, as part of my job, to travel to most places. It is that which made it essential that we should not allow it to be spoilt.

Whilst the Directorate was administering it we were, I think, successful in preventing unwelcome access. This was helped by its remoteness which also meant we could monitor potential intruders long before they got there.

During the Directorate's administration, we recorded only a limited number of incursions. The occasional cruise ship which once intercepted normally moved off without argument. A few lone individuals, mainly photographers, managed to creep in but we believe caused no long term interference. The poachers were a bit more serious but we don't think they had any influence on the problems we are now here to discuss.

There were periods, some long, of significant climate change which affected differing parts of the Reserve. There were for instance times when there was considerable expansion of the ice cap so it covered and obliterated about a third of the area of the Reserve. There were some periods of drought, particularly near the centre, causing desert conditions and there were times of fluctuation in sea levels, sometimes reducing and sometimes increasing the land area. All these had effects on the landscape, but were agreed to be a normal part of natural change and not due to external influences and not something we could or should interfere with.

Following Idreji's appointment as Administrators the Directorate was limited to a supervisory and regulatory role – mainly formal pre-notified periodic Inspections as stipulated in Idreji's contract.

The Inspection reports received showed little out of the normal. The arrangements seemed to be working and Retha appeared mainly undisturbed.

In fact nothing really untoward was formally reported until the most recent periodic inspection by Chief Warden Avsa Signe which showed up very disturbing changes and damage to the Reserve. I must say in all honesty that the Department has to accept some blame for the longer than usual delay between this Inspection and the previous one. This was made worse by the fact that that previous Inspection was carried out by a team who had no previous knowledge of Retha and were therefore possibly less equipped to detect changes before they became serious. To blame budget cuts is an easy excuse but in this case it is a true one.

As many will be aware, Avsa Signe was the very original Warden of Retha. In fact his involvement goes back long before then. He was part of the original team from the Directorate that mapped and catalogued it. It was he who guided the original Inspector round the Reserve. He was formally appointed Warden as soon as the Protected Status was confirmed. He remained at the Reserve until Idreji took over and was then posted away. It is true to say that that was at Idreji's request which in hindsight my predecessor should probably not have agreed to.

Advokate Otto Slaborg.   Inspector I really must protest.   That is a totally irrelevant and improper comment.

Inspector. Noted. Please continue Director.

Director Erigh Jonsen.   Chief Warden Signe's recent Inspection was the first time he had returned to Retha since Idreji took over. One of the reasons I chose him to lead this Inspection was that we had received some disturbing anecdotal evidence of problems at Retha. This could just have been gossip but I thought it was best not only to have a senior Warden carry out the Inspection but also one who knew the Reserve intimately and would have no problem in noticing any changes.

As I assume everyone is aware Avsa was very seriously injured during that visit. Without the brave actions of his son, Warden Olte Signe and of Sub Warden Prima Sven, he would certainly have died. As it is they managed to extricate him with great difficulty and bring him back to Base. They were then eventually able to transfer him to a hospital, where he is recovering, but it is unlikely that he will ever be fully mobile again.

Warden Olte Signe and Sub Warden Prima Sven submitted a report as soon as they could and on the strength of that the Directorate called for an emergency conference with Idreji at which it was ultimately, after some discussion, agreed that we should call for this

Inquiry. It was also agreed that the Directorate would take back the administration of the Reserve. I have appointed Olte Signe to be the Warden and he and Sub Warden Sven will be taking over there as soon as they have got their team together.

Olte has now prepared a detailed Inspection report for this Inquiry. We hope that Avsa Signe may be able to add his own report, either recorded or by link from the hospital, but we are not sure he will be well enough.

We have also commissioned a number of specialist reports and some more have come in independently, mainly from members or former members of the University of Idreji. The Inquiry should have received those already. At least one more is awaited. We are in fact currently having difficulty communicating with Professor Andemus, who many of you will know from her books and programmes, but hopefully this is simply because of the reception problems that are inevitable in her field of work.

Private Journal

I found I was shaking when I read this. I stopped for a while adjusting from the sudden pleasure of hearing from Avsa after half a life time and that yes he did have a son, to then hearing that he was never likely to recover from what seemed to be horrific injuries.

I couldn't imagine Avsa crippled. He was the one who could go anywhere. He was the one everyone else could rely on. He got to places more quickly than anyone else which is an enormous advantage in a job that has to cope with such vast distances. He had been the very opposite of the somewhat protected, studious, legal and bureaucratic community I was used to.

I couldn't get my head round the timing. I knew from Avsa's message that the Inquiry had been some time ago but how long I couldn't work out from the file in front of me. I messaged Peti and asked her to find out what she could. Was he still alive? Was he still in Hospital? I told her to try to keep her enquiries as low key as possible. As an afterthought I also asked her to find out what she could about the son.

She came back very quickly to say that she'd been able to trace the hospital he'd been taken to and that she had managed to access his records. He had been in intensive care for a long time but was still alive and now out of danger. He was virtually paralysed on his left side. His humerus, ulna and radius on that side had all been badly damaged. She said he was still in the same hospital which was apparently little more than a mobile Expedition Accident Unit. It had obviously looked after him well when he was first brought in but it wasn't equipped for long term remedial therapy and she was surprised he was still there. He only had limited mobility and was never likely to be able to travel again unassisted.

I asked her to see if she could find out anymore. Whether he needed further treatment and if so where he could go and whether that was feasible.

Director Erigh Jonsen (contd).   To summarise the reports we have received, there seems no doubt that very substantial damage has been caused to the Reserve.   This has apparently been done over a surprisingly short period.   Virtually the whole of the Reserve appears to have been affected to a greater or lesser extent.

There has been widespread destruction of the forests which is what is most obvious visually. Very large areas of land have been cleared.   We also have reports of pollution of water courses and of the sea. The evidence you will hear will go into this in more detail. The result seems to have been not only extensive damage to the environment and landscape, but also widespread death and destruction of species of all kinds in the Reserve. From the information we have, the animal population as a whole has been reduced by at least half and many species now appear to be completely extinct or close to extinction.   This loss of species is estimated to be between one hundred and one thousand times more than the natural rate of extinction.   That represents thousands and thousands of species over a very short period. Most of it apparently since the last Inspection.

It is our duty as Applicants to provide evidence of that destruction and where the responsibility lies, but as I understand it that is not likely to be in dispute. What I think may be disputed is our conclusion that a Section 427 Order is the only remedy.

MESSAGE

From: Warden O Signe

To: Chief Warden A Signe

How are you? The Inquiry has just started. The Inspector is an old stick but he seems OK. The Director has finished his opening submissions. Idreji have a Lawyer. He's on next. Talk here is that when the Director got mine and Prima's report he went ballistic. That must have been because of what happened to you. Anyway he got straight onto Professor Whatsis name at Idreji but got nowhere. So he just flew there and insisted on seeing the Dean and demanded a joint application for an immediate Inquiry and wouldn't give up until they agreed. He also got them to agree to give back the Administration and he has put me and Prima into the Reserve as Wardens. We were right, they don't have any people there! They certainly appear pretty defensive. Did Idreji do all this deliberately or did they just mess it up? Is it an experiment that went wrong? I'm on shortly. Wish me luck. **Olte.**

COUNCIL of COMMISSIONERS

Retha Inquiry Transcript CONTINUED

Inspector. I now invite Advokate Otto Slaborg to make his opening submissions.

Advokate Otto Slaborg. Thank you Inspector. I will be very brief. By way of introduction I am a Member of the Bar of the Commonwealth of Idreji and am also authorised as an Advocate by the Council of Commissioners.

As I have said I am instructed by the University of Idreji to act for them in this Inquiry. A number of the members and ex members of the University have independently given notice of their wish to give evidence on the scientific issues.

My role is simply to represent the University's own interests. As is widely known there have been a number of wild and unsubstantiated criticisms made against the University in respect of its handling of the Retha Administration. Whilst the University accepts that there are matters that might have been undertaken better, they strongly resent and refute the wider implications of irregularity and impropriety and I will not hesitate to object if those are raised and will demand the opportunity to respond.

MESSAGE

From: Chief Warden A Signe

To: Warden O Signe

Congratulations on the promotion! As you know I always hoped you would take over Retha. I wish it was in happier circumstances but if you can't do it, no-one can.

I am fine. They say I won't be able to move properly again but we'll see about that. I'm still bed bound but hopefully they'll disconnect me from all the apparatus soon so I can start moving a bit.

I don't think Idreji caused this deliberately.

Personally I think they were just incompetent and arrogant and when it started going wrong they didn't know what to do. I think we'd have just sorted it before it got to be a legal problem. I don't think they had any idea of running a Reserve. They just saw it as a research plaything.

Don't worry about giving evidence, you'll be fine. **Da**

Inspector. If there are no other opening submissions I will now move onto Section Two. The first Witness is Warden Olte Signe. You should all have received a copy of his detailed report. You can raise such comments or questions as you wish at the end but if they are in respect of a particular part of his report and you would like them raised when he reaches that point please message me as soon as you can.

Warden Olte Signe. Chief Warden Avsa Signe, Sub Warden Prima Sven and myself were instructed by the Director to carry out an Inspection of Retha on behalf of the Directorate. As has been said Chief Warden Avsa Signe was well acquainted with Retha. So was I. I was born on the Retha base and lived there whilst my father was Warden. It was Sub Warden Prima Sven's first visit.

We commenced our inspection as usual at the latitudinal centre of the Reserve and intended to fly straight round at maximum altitude. This way you get a good overview in a short time with the minimum risk of disturbance to the indigenous birds and animals.

We came in first over the sea. There were no immediate reasons for concern except we did encounter areas of debris – some quite large – on our initial approach to the Reserve which we left for investigation later. To be honest we just wanted to get there. It was a long time since either I or my father had been back.

We made landfall at the mouth of a large river in the temperate zone. We realised immediately something was wrong. We had expected to see natural changes.

A large Reserve like Retha is constantly changing. An area that was previously savannah becomes rain forest or vice versa. Rivers change course. Sea levels go up and down. The size of ice caps can change dramatically. But this was something different.

The sky was fairly cloudy and we couldn't get a good view initially so we circled round a bit.

In an area like that we would have expected to see mainly marsh and mudflats which would be supporting an enormous variety of wildlife. The slightly higher ground behind should have been wooded with occasional areas of heath or grassland.

Instead it had been completely changed. The landscape had been divided up into a patchwork of areas of different colours. There were alien structures or buildings of some kind dotted all over, some in very large groups. The river shape wasn't natural. The outflow was discoloured.

We went a bit further to see how far all this went, by then the clouds had cleared a bit. It was much the same as far as we could see. In fact it seemed to get worse the further we went on.

The woods were gone. Entire natural valleys and forests had just been obliterated.

Private Journal

I got a second message from Peti "Sorry I forgot to mention the son. That's taking a bit longer. I'll come back as soon as I can. I am still trying to find out about moving the Chief Warden to a bigger hospital but I think it will be difficult."

She came back quite quickly. "All I can find out is that Chief Warden Signe isn't married and isn't believed to be in a relationship. Apparently the son just appeared as a baby at the Reserve Base. Chief Warden Signe never explained how or why. He brought him up single handed. He has always been treated as his son. Whether he's actually his, or a relative's or a friend's no-one knows.

Warden Olte Signe (contd).   We thought the best thing to do was to continue a high level observation of the whole Reserve. We circled it three times. Whilst there were areas that seemed less affected by whatever it was we were seeing, there were very few places that hadn't suffered some damage. The ice areas seemed least affected as did the areas immediately adjoining them.

Although we were still at a very great height we began to work out what had changed. The scale of the deforestation was beyond belief. In the temperate areas there was very little left. In the rainforest, what my father used to call the Lungs of Retha, there were now huge areas of open land where previously there would have been uninterrupted boundless tracts of forest.   We assumed initially that this must have been caused by disease, fire or climate change. When we were later able to look at it in greater detail we realised that most of the cleared areas were being cultivated.   Scattered around were these groups of structures or buildings. Every now and again there was a much larger concentrated grouping which blanketed the countryside.

We had intended to sleep outside on Retha. It wasn't strictly permitted in the past but we knew how and where we could safely do it without disturbing the native species.   This time the more we looked the more we realised it would be impossible to land safely until we knew what all this was, so we went to the base. There was no-one there which we found suspicious. We had expected the Idrejians to be there.

That night we discussed in detail what we had seen, what we thought had caused it and what we should do. We assumed at that stage that this was the work of a colonising species alien to Retha.

None of us had any experience of urban civilisations having lived and worked on reserves all our lives so we didn't, at that stage, know exactly what we were looking at.

We checked the equipment we had on the base to see if there was anything which would give us a better view but all we came across were two elderly magnifying cameras.

When we ran it the Base had a full inventory of observation equipment. They were our major monitoring tools. With them we could see virtually everything on the land surface in detail. The only areas we had difficulty with were the oceans and the forests. Obviously we weren't physically able to get into either of them. We could have dropped monitoring devices which would have sent back images and sound and given some feel for what was down there, but they were dismissed because we couldn't have recovered them and they would have been there for ever. Eventually we adopted the practice of hovering over the surface of the ocean or forest and dropping smaller monitors in on lines and pulling them up when we were done. The main risk was if they got caught on an obstruction but we always managed to disentangle them. The worst time was when a large fish swallowed one and father had to play it until it was exhausted and we could haul it up and remove the monitor. At least we were able to get a close view of that fish before we dropped it back!

None of this equipment was left. One of the cameras was defective but we got the other one working. By then the Reserve was out of view so we settled down for the night and waited for it to come in sight again next day.

We then focussed the camera on the largest areas of whatever we were seeing. We took as many photos as we could, at as great a magnification as the equipment allowed.

Even with the magnification of the camera, we could only see major changes, not the detail. We could see where the forests had been cleared. We could see that the landscape had altered and that things which, as I say we assumed were buildings, now covered the land but what exactly they were we couldn't make out.

We agreed that we would send all the photographs we had taken back to Head Office so they could do what they could to enhance them and get more detail.

I understand Senior Technician Nand from the Directorate will be showing all those photos and his interpretation of them in his Report but I thought it might help if I included a couple here. We think we have been able to identify images that were taken of the same place in the past.

That is what we think it used to look like. This is what it looks like now.

Private Journal

I looked at the first set of photos. Despite all that length of time I thought I recognised it.

I and Avsa had been away for much longer than planned. I think it was expected we would only be gone a couple of days. Somehow there was always something new to look at and we started going further and further. We fed and slept each night where we stopped.

At first I was worried whether we should be getting back. I tried to communicate with the Director but the further we went the more difficult the communication seemed to be and eventually we gave up and just enjoyed ourselves. After all who was going to complain?

It was the first and possibly the only time in my life I have ever felt free to do what I liked.

Each morning Avsa would say he wanted to show me something new and we'd go off in that direction. One day it was enormous expanses of sea and ice. Avsa was constantly pointing things out. Big grey sea animals hauled out on the ice. Funny solemn upright birds that would suddenly jump into the sea. I think Avsa showed me over twenty different kinds of them. Then he was showing me immense seabirds that never approached land except to breed and spent all the rest of their lives permanently in the air. Then I or he would see something completely different and we'd go off at a tangent to look at it.

One day when we were flying back to the warmer middle area we came down low along a coastline. Sandy beaches as far as you could see with salt lagoons behind. By this time I had got used to both the number, and differing types of the birds which shared the sky with us.

Avsa kept telling me about what we saw. The tiny little low flying dark birds, with the swept back wings, that flew each year from the other end of Retha to the same place just to breed. The distances they flew were quite unbelievable for something that small. They would breed, hatch and fledge their chicks and then all fly back together to their other world for winter only to do it all over again the following year.

He told me about the little white and grey sea birds with the black heads. Each year the male would return just before his mate, to the exact beach where his parents and their parents had always bred, to get everything ready. His mate would then fly in to that exact spot even though she hadn't seen him since the last summer and they would breed, produce their offspring and separate again. How could they possibly know when or where to go?

Eventually we turned up this wide river mouth. I don't suppose it was as spectacular as some of the things we had seen but there was a quiet beauty about it. Woodland and streams and meadow and marsh. I thought it was heaven.

Then I turned to the new photos. I had difficulty identifying how they related to the first ones. All the woods had gone. The river was a different colour. Its shape had been changed. There were vast buildings and structures along it. There were tracks all over the place. The beauty had gone and so had the birds and animals. Something had taken one of the most beautiful places in the Universe and had destroyed it. Why?

Warden Olte Signe (contd).   We then debated what to do next.   When my father ran the Reserve he would make low level flights as a matter of course, even though the guidance rules said that strictly we should try to keep to a height at which we could not be observed and would not disturb the wildlife.

He said you could get a better feel for what was going on, on flights like that. His skill was to know when it was safe to drop down and when not. I think the problem is that Idreji can't have done any of this so they didn't notice what was happening until it was too late.

Advokate Otto Slaborg.   I protest, that is pure conjecture and totally unsubstantiated.

Inspector. Noted.

Warden Olte Signe   Sub Warden Prima Sven has better eyesight than me or my father. She comes from Hatoban. Whilst my father and I were talking she had kept looking through the camera lens. She said she thought she could see movement above the surface of the Reserve. Big things. Much larger than birds, moving around very fast.

It seemed stupid to come all that way without trying to see a bit more. We decided to go out again at a lower height, but still not less than half altitude. This would give us a bit better view, but would still mean we would be hardly be visible from the surface and be well above these things flying around.

We went further to where the plains start. When we had been there last this was one vast expanse of prairie with occasional wooded mountain ranges, rivers and lakes. At first we thought nothing had changed but as we lost height and could pick up a bit more detail we realised the land looked different. It was now divided up to form large uniform parcels, mainly covered by crops we didn't recognise, stretching away into the distance. Further on where the terrain changes we could see, if we looked carefully, that there were enormous herds of animals grazing but they weren't the animals that had been there before. These were slow moving, lethargic creatures. There was none of the movement and vibrancy of the great herds we used to see.

In the distance we then saw a smoke haze and as we got closer we realised it was a vast creeping sprawl of buildings, just dropped into the middle of the plains.

We were worried about getting too close particularly as we didn't know what was there but we dropped down just a little so we could make out a bit more. Even at that height we could hear constant noise coming up from whatever was down there. The air had an unpleasant smell. When we flew back later, it was in the dark but there were thousands of lights of some kind shining up at us.

Private Journal

I couldn't be sure if I remembered that exact place. It was a long time ago and we saw so much. I certainly remember those vast plains, totally unspoilt, left as they had been for ever. What I did remember was the dark brown clouds on the surface which at first seemed to be static and then you realised they were enormous herds of large shaggy brown animals. All slowly moving in one gigantic mass. We followed one for half a day and never tired of the magic of it.

I looked at the recent photos and couldn't see any of these animals. They had gone as had their boundless unspoilt plains.

Warden Olte Signe (contd).   The next day we just flew over the sea. This had always been safer because there was very little below to see you. If you position yourself in the right way you can view the land beyond with little risk of disturbing any of the indigenous creatures.

Chief Warden Signe then indicated he was going to make a low level flight along the coastline and that we were to go up to a safe altitude and wait. We saw him fly into the distance. At that height he could see anything on the water and get a good view of the coast as well.

My father was gone a long time and we became worried. We dropped height a bit and flew in the direction we had last seen him. This was a coastline he and I both knew well. I had flown along it hundreds of times. Apart from a rocky headland and a few islands there was nothing in the way.

We tried to raise contact with him but there was nothing. We flew on uneventfully. Then suddenly out of nowhere something blasted past us at great speed. Fortunately I and Sub Warden Sven were flying some way apart and it passed between us narrowly missing her. It was larger than any bird I've seen. It flew off into the distance before we could work out what it was.

Before we could recover, another one of these things did the same. This time we were a bit further away and got a better view. It had wings, but they didn't move. It made a lot of noise. It disturbed the air all around it. For a long time afterwards you could still feel the turbulence it caused.

We gained height and circled round and eventually saw that these things were flying out from a large flat area just by the coast, at the edge of one of these built up areas. They seemed to be flying in and out all the time.

We tried to establish contact with my father again and this time got a weak signal. We followed it as best we could but could only maintain contact by dropping altitude. We found ourselves getting closer and closer to this flying place.

At that moment Prima shouted that she could see something in the water. We circled round while we tried to work out what to do. We began to realise these flying things always flew in and out in exactly the same direction so there were areas in which they did not fly. We manoeuvred ourselves round until we were sure it was safe and I dropped down to sea level to see if I could make out what Sub Warden Sven had seen.

The sea was pretty rough and visibility at that level wasn't good but after some searching I saw my father in the water. I landed by him. He was conscious but very badly hurt. I signalled to Prima and she came down. My father couldn't move. He is a lot bigger than either of us but eventually we lifted him up and flew him back to Base and managed to give him emergency first aid. Luckily there was a mobile accident hospital run by the Medicali Foundation not too far away and we were eventually able to transfer him to it. If it hadn't been for them he wouldn't be alive now.

All we could do then was send our reports and the photos to Head Office.

Inspector. Thank you. I have received comments and questions for Warden Signe from President Henk O Kang of the Universal Wildlife Protection Fund and from Advokate Otto Slaborg for the University of Idreji.

President Henk O Kang. Can I say how distressed we were to hear of your Father's injuries. We pray that he will recover and return to his life's work. He is one of the greats. He has done more for conservation than probably any other living being. Do you know what caused his injuries?

Warden Olte Signe. Thank you. I'll pass what you say on to him. I think he still doesn't know what hit him. The first he remembers is when he woke up in the sea.

Advokate Otto Slaborg. Do you personally know what species has caused this damage to Retha?

Warden Olte Signe. No.

Advokate Otto Slaborg. From your own inspections were you able to tell whether this damage has been caused by an indigenous, introduced or colonising species?

Warden Olte Signe. No.

Advokate Otto Slaborg. Are you suggesting that the University of Idreji is in anyway responsible.

Warden Olte Signe. I cannot answer that.

Director Erigh Jonsen. Although Warden Olte Signe was too modest to mention it, the journey back to the base was long and difficult. Not only had he and Sub Warden Sven the weight of his father to carry but they also had to avoid the debris they had previously observed. Warden Signe himself was injured in one collision, though thankfully not too seriously and he has now fully recovered.

By way of explanation, after we had processed the photos, I went to discuss the matter with our colleagues on Idreji. It was agreed that there would need to be an Inquiry and that we should jointly notify the Council immediately to get things underway. In the meantime the Dean of Idreji agreed to co-operate as far as they could although they apparently no longer had a Resident Warden team there.

We were fortunate to be able to arrange with the Ringooen Navy for one of its unmanned survey buoys to do a circle of the Reserve to see if it could provide better photos than those that Chief Warden Signe and his team were able to take. We also asked them to investigate the report of debris above the Reserve.

This left the seas and oceans as the main gap in our investigations and we were lucky that Professor Andemus was doing some filming not that far away and volunteered to carry out a sub aqua inspection. She is of course better equipped to do this than anyone else and she and her team have sent back some useful material. However as I said we are now out of contact with her which is causing some concern.

Once we were able to put all our findings together and had had the opportunity to analyse them and the various photos that had been taken, we then felt that we had sufficient evidence to initiate the Inquiry.

Private Journal

I found I could hardly breath I was so upset. Retha had been the most wonderful experience I have ever had. In a life circumscribed by convention and rules and duty it was my one moment of freedom. The opportunity to do what I wanted. A place which I will always remember as unbelievably beautiful. Who or what could possibly have done this to Avsa of all people. He had given up most of his life to Retha. I was furious with Idreji, angry with whatever had done it.

MESSAGE
From: Warden O Signe
To: Chief Warden A Signe

I've given my evidence. It seemed to go OK. The President of the UWPF said some very nice things about you and asked about your injuries and who or what had caused them. Have you worked out yet what hit you? How are you getting on? What do the Doctors think?

The Lawyer for Idreji asked whether the species that has done the damage to the Reserve is indigenous, colonisers or introduced. I said I didn't know. **Olte**

Director Erigh Jonsen (contd).   I will now call Senior Technician Nand of the Directorate.

Senior Technician Nand.   I am the Head of the Conservation Directorate's Technical Division.   I received, from our Inspection team on Retha, a large number of undeveloped photos for analysis and interpretation. These had been taken on a very old camera which is no longer in general service.   I had never come across its type before and I had some difficulty extracting and developing the pictures.   My instructions were to enhance them as far as was possible and analyse what could be seen. I was given, for comparison purposes, photographs of the same or similar locations that had been taken by previous teams. I was later given photos that had been taken by the Ringooen Navy's unmanned buoy, which provided more detail in some places.

It is probably helpful if I start with the general analysis of the changes that can be seen to the whole planet and then move on to closer examination of specific areas.

The change in forestation is the most obvious. Comparing the previous photos with all the current ones it can be seen that very significant reductions in forested areas have taken place.   I estimate these have now been reduced by between fifty and seventy percent.

The areas that have been cleared are being used mainly for what appears to be intensive crop cultivation. I am not a botanical expert but I couldn't find any evidence of these crops in the previous photos. They appear to have been introduced recently and artificially.

There are also large areas of livestock which are in fenced areas and would seem to be farmed, rather than wild, animals. The areas and numbers of these animals is enormous and I can only assume they are being farmed to eat though I repeat, this is not my field of expertise. Where the forests still remain we saw, on the photos, big fires burning which would seem to be a way these forests are being cleared. As well as destroying the trees this must also be killing large numbers of the creatures living in those forests. It is certainly wiping out their natural habitat.

There are groups of what we all agree are buildings dotted everywhere. The ones we looked at initially were in comparatively small groups. Then occasionally there was a larger grouping. We were able to magnify some of those photos sufficiently to identify more clearly what they consisted of. Generally there were roofed buildings of different shapes and kinds. Some were quite large. Some were just single storey shacks. We could just make out creatures walking in and out. Most of the views we got were very blurred but they appeared to be bipeds - erect and walking on two legs.

We then started looking at the photos of the much larger sprawl of these buildings in the temperate zone which Chief Warden Signe and his team photographed. Here we were able to obtain a better clarity of magnification.

This is a large sprawling conurbation made up of thousands of individual buildings. These buildings are roofed and again appear to have different heights and sizes and possibly different uses. Some are very large and tall. Some have little spaces, normally green, round them. Some are joined onto the buildings on either side. They are connected up by networks of artificial tracks. These tracks join other tracks which join yet more tracks, some large. We looked to see what was using them. We could see little boxes, which we assumed were conveyances of some kind, moving along them which certainly weren't natural. We saw that when these boxes stopped creatures got out. In other words they were using these boxes to get about. We blew up the photos of these creatures as much as we could. As we had guessed previously, they stood vertically on two legs which leaves their forelegs and forepaws free.

We were later able to identify that there were a number of different types of these moving conveyances. Some were the small ones, some were similar but a lot larger and some were what seemed to be long snakes of them.

This large conurbation had no crops that we could see. This must mean the creatures' food is brought in from outside. Maybe in the larger conveyances. What the creatures did we could not tell but there were thousands, no hundreds of thousands, of them.

The river was disturbed and badly discoloured. There were outfalls of polluted water running into it. If you look at the earlier photos the whole area has changed. The river shape is different, most of the marshes have been built over and there is little or no wildlife.

Private Journal

There should have been the vast flocks of large waterbirds on the marsh and flying above. There should have been waders on the mudflats and in the shallow water. There should have been divers in the creeks and marshes. One day Avsa counted thirteen different species of divers. There should have been small herds of animals on the marsh. There should have been predatory animals prowling around and birds of prey hovering overhead.

Over the time we spent out on the Reserve we probably stopped here, or at least somewhere very similar, as often as anywhere else. It was the summer in those parts. The days were longer and warm. We were woken each morning to the sound of movement around us. The smaller birds were all singing – something they seemed to do at dawn and dusk. The gigantic flocks of waterbirds squabbled and squawked. Then suddenly one immense group would take off and wheel round and round until everyone had joined and they would then fly off to that day's feeding grounds. One bird in the lead and all the others in a V shape behind. How they could get that organised, apparently so effortlessly, I couldn't imagine. We normally go off one after the other in a line. The seals on the sandbanks would start their strange mewing. The little waders who fed on the mud flats would come alive as the tide fell and start feeding for the day. Ducks of differing varieties would suddenly be out on the water, diving and splashing around. On our first couple of visits seabirds were nesting on the shingle sitting on their eggs. In some places you couldn't walk without disturbing something.

There were brown long tailed animals swimming in the river and tiny bright blue and orange birds flying fast, straight and low over the ponds from one fishing point to the next. When it got dark you heard the call of birds hunting across the marshes and animals barking and growling. One night just as it got dark an enormous herd of deer, some with magnificent antlers, came down to the fresh water ponds to drink.

Once in the late afternoon a cloud of smallish dark coloured birds appeared over the reed beds. They moved as one living swirling cloud, its shape constantly changing. The cloud got bigger and bigger as more birds joined. Every now and again this enormous swarm would move down, almost touching the ground as if it was going to land. Then it would take off again and swoop around overhead. This went on for some time until suddenly the whole cloud funnelled down and was sucked into the marsh, like a reverse tornado, and they were gone for the night.

MESSAGE

From: Chief Warden A Signe

To: Warden O Signe

*No I still can't work out what I hit. One moment I was flying along and the next I remember I was in the water and then you turned up. I can't remember any noise or warning. Personally I don't think it was something that flew into me. I think it was something I flew into but what could be out there on the sea which I didn't notice I don't know. I suppose I must have been concentrating on the coast and can't have been looking at what was in front of me. Whatever it was it wasn't there when we ran the Reserve. **Da***

Senior Technician Nand (contd). We were able to view the flying objects Warden Olte Signe referred to. This is one of the photos. You will see it is a large winged machine with what must be propellant engines. They would appear, from what we can see on other photos, to take hundreds of these creatures.

We can't tell from still images where and how far they go but it would seem as though they need a flat area to take off from and that they must be used for going longer distances particularly over water. We guess the moving boxes, which stay on the ground and use the tracks, are used for shorter distances. It seems to suggest that not only is this species not very mobile on land but also that it cannot fly or swim - at least for any long distances.

The fact that they are comparatively immobile may be the reason why they need these built up areas to live and work in.

Our photos also showed metal towers with wires between them running across the countryside and other tall towers with moving arms. We also had some photos of the sea, particularly close to the coast. Those also showed the tall towers with moving arms which may be what injured Chief Warden Signe. There were also very large boxes moving on the water. We think that they must be this creature's way of transporting things on the sea from one place to another but why they would want to do this we couldn't tell.

Inspector. Thank you. The only questions for Senior Technician Nand are from Advokate Otto Slaborg.

Advokate Otto Slaborg. Do you personally know what species has caused this damage to Retha?

Senior Technician Nand. I am satisfied it is the biped species we identified.

Advokate Otto Slaborg. Do you know whether the species is indigenous, introduced or external colonisers?

Senior Technician Nand. No.

Advokate Otto Slaborg. Are you suggesting that the University of Idreji is in anyway responsible.

Senior Technician Nand. I have no idea.

Inspector. The next witness is Professor Quvvon, formerly a lecturer in the Department of Nature Conservation at the University of Idreji and now Professor of Conservation Studies at the Cormact Institute.

Professor Quvvon. Thank you. I was contacted by the Director and asked to make a report for this Inquiry. My speciality study, when I was at Idreji, was in the tropical rainforests of Retha. There are two other eco systems, of which we are aware, which have some similarity to the Retha rainforests but Retha's are by far the largest, most developed and until now most unspoilt.

I was fortunate enough to be appointed part of the permanent team when the University took over the Reserve. At that time we had the advantage that the Directorate had left behind some very sophisticated monitoring systems which it had developed.

Subsequently we had the benefit of significant new funding which enabled the University to increase the scale and performance of those systems. I have never worked with such advanced equipment before or since. I gather that that funding dried up some time ago.

The problem, as has already been said, is that even with that equipment, it was difficult to see into the rain forest. After some research it was decided that I would concentrate my studies on one specific area on a large island just a little short of the middle of the planet. We devised a capsule in which two of us could stay for as long as we wanted. It was designed to cause the minimum disturbance to the indigenous wildlife and vegetation. We stationed it next to a river which meant we could get it in without much difficulty and similarly recover it when we had finished. It enabled us to monitor movements above us, at ground level and along the river in detail. The limitation was that we had to wait for things to come to us!

We were there for fifty of Retha's years which is a short period in terms of our own life span. During that time we counted and identified literally thousands of different animals from large mammals to snakes, tiny insects and birds of amazing varieties. That area was quite the most prolific habitat I have ever heard of even by Retha's standards. It was a lesson not just in conservation and species identification but also in advanced evolution. We could see how everything had adapted to that specific environment.

This was a totally unspoilt eco system brimming in variety, both zoological and botanical, in perfect balance. It had developed over history to become what one can only describe as a perfect living macrocosm. It and the other rainforests have a dominating effect on the well

53

being of the whole planet. They are quite the most extraordinary and diverse environments you could find. There were probably hundreds of thousands of different creatures and plants which have taken eons to develop and have now apparently been destroyed in what is, in terms of the Universe, just a blink of an eye.

We were not able to study the flora in as great a detail as the animal life simply because of our stationary position and the very short visibility you have in forests of this nature. Even so we were able to identify hundreds of separate species.

After that programme ended I was posted back to the main base where I was put in charge of observing and mapping the other forests.

At that time the tropical, temperate and high altitude forests took up about seventy percent of the entire land surface of the planet. Apart from the occasional fire, there was no significant damage or change whilst I was there.

We did identify some ocean and climatic changes which had affected some of the forests in the past but none in my time. There was occasional sporadic volcanic activity but this tended to be localised. I suspect that if there was a spectacular eruption over a protracted period the clouds could have had a significant detrimental affect but this didn't happen whilst I was there and there was no evidence of any recent occurrence.

We took it for granted that these forests would continue to remain undisturbed so I was very concerned when I received the reports about Retha from the Director. He passed me the photos Chief Warden Avsa Signe and his team had taken and also the more advanced ones taken by the Ringooen Navy.

I calculate that the total area of the temperate forest has been reduced by ninety percent since I left and the rainforest by around half. Most of the damage to the rainforest appears very recent. It seems to have been wholesale thoughtless destruction. Nothing seems to have been done to protect the species there. For instance to ensure they have corridors from one of the diminishing areas of forest that remain to the others. It seems to have happened in a very short while. The cleared areas have been taken over for intensive crop cultivation in most part. There also seems to be domestic animal rearing in some areas and some have been left waste maybe because they were just cleared for their timber.

I can only guess at the damage this must be having to the whole planet in terms of air quality, rainfall, temperature and ocean levels. You can't just take out that amount of forest. The damage to all the wildlife must be terrible.

From the photos I've seen I couldn't identify exactly what had caused this destruction. It appeared to me that a species, possibly more than one, but I suspect only one, has expanded its population so quickly that it has taken over more and more of the Reserve's surface to live in and to cultivate crops. I guess that what we are looking at in these photos is split into areas in which they live and those they grow their food in. They have limited mobility but they are clearly capable of building and manufacturing things.

There was certainly no species capable of doing this whilst I was on Retha.

Inspector.   Thank you Professor Quvvon.   I think there are just questions from Advokate Otto Slaborg.

Advokate Otto Slaborg.   Do you personally know what species has caused this damage to Retha?

Professor Quvvon.   No.

Advokate Otto Slaborg.   Do you know whether the species is indigenous, introduced or external colonisers?

Professor Quvvon.   No.

Advokate Otto Slaborg.   Are you suggesting that the University of Idreji is in anyway responsible?

Professor Quvvon.   Not as far as I am aware.

MESSAGE

From: Warden O Signe

To: Chief Warden A Signe

Min Nand and a Professor from Idreji have given their evidence. The Professor, I think he may be working somewhere else now, was very good. They do seem to have done some very detailed research into the rainforest whilst he was there.

The Lawyer from Idreji asked the same questions he asked me. He must be making some legal point.

The Director said that it was you who took the Inspector, who carried out the first inspection, round – is that right? **Olte**

From: Chief Warden A Signe

To: Warden O Signe

Yes. **Da**

From: Warden O Signe

To: Chief Warden A Signe

You never mentioned that before. **Olte**

From: Chief Warden A Signe

To: Warden O Signe

No. **Da.**

From: Warden O Signe

To: Chief Warden A Signe

The Director said the Inspection went on for some time. Was there a reason? **Olte**

From: Chief Warden A Signe
To: Warden O Signe
We just spent a long time down there. ***Da***

From: Warden O Signe
To: Chief Warden A Signe
What was the Inspector like? ***Olte***

From: Chief Warden A Signe
To: Warden O Signe
She was the most beautiful thing I have ever seen.
Da

From: Warden O Signe
To: Chief Warden A Signe
Is that all? ***Olte***

Private Journal

I was told I was going to do this Inspection. All of us Commissioners had to do some ground visits as part of our training. Journeys of that kind were much more difficult then and it took a very long time to get there. That was another reason for sending us youngsters. Thankfully there have been lots of improvements in star navigation since. I finally reached the ship which they were using as their temporary base. The Director came out to greet me. I was tired, dirty and hungry but he propelled me into this smallish room which was full of staff from all over the Cosmos. It was a bit overwhelming. They stopped talking as soon as I walked in.

The Director tried to introduce everyone to me but it was too much to take in. The last person he introduced was Avsa, who had been standing at the back.

MESSAGE

From: Chief Warden A Signe
To: Warden O Signe

We were told an Inspector was arriving to decide on the Application for Protected Status. We were all in the temporary mess room waiting. Then the Director walked in with the Inspector behind him. The Director introduced her in a rather embarrassed way and then invited her to talk. I don't think he'd expected a Commissioner.

I don't remember one word of what she said I was just mesmerised. We all were. I suppose that was her skill. I just remember her talking to us in the quiet assured manner she had.

When she finished the Director thanked her and said that she had asked to see as much of Retha as possible. He turned to me and said that he suggested I would be the best person to act as her guide.

He had mentioned this to me earlier when we had been preparing for the visit but that was when we were all expecting a middle aged bureaucrat. This wasn't what I had planned for. I was completely in awe. I had never met anything like her. She had a serene beauty which is impossible to describe.

She was obviously important but I did not know exactly who she was. I'd no idea how you treated someone like that. What would she expect? Would she be happy coming out with me on our own?

It took us that day to get ready. I asked her if there was anything particular she wanted to see. She replied, in the way she had which made you feel important, that she was happy to leave that to me so that's what I did. **Da**

COUNCIL of COMMISSIONERS

Retha Inquiry Transcript CONTINUED

Director. The next witness is Commander Ratohnen of the Ringooen Navy who because of his other duties has submitted a recorded report.

Commander Ratohnen. I was instructed at the request of the Directorate of Conservation to arrange for our nearest unmanned survey buoy to take what photos it could of the surface of Retha, with as much magnification as was possible. We were also asked to see if we could identify reported debris which had been found on the approach to Retha.

It took us a little while to manoeuvre the buoy into optimum position. Most of the images of the surface were not as good as we had hoped but were the best we could manage. There were a few that were very good and showed significant detail. I have attached them to this report. You will see there are some quite good close ups of the urban areas including individual buildings. There are two that give very good shots of the bipeds that seemed to be living in them. We passed on all the photos we took to the Directorate's technical people for them to analyse and interpret for themselves and they are submitting their own report.

We had a bit more success with the reported debris simply because there was clearer visibility at that height. There seems to be a continuous haze of some kind in the atmosphere immediately above the Reserve which distorts visibility. This dissipates the further out you get so its easier to get a clearer view.

The whole outer atmosphere of the planet is littered with metallic rubbish. I have never seen anything like it before. It is as if it's being used as a rubbish tip. I attach photos. It will be seen that the pieces vary from tiny fragments to quite large complete units of some kind. It will make future access to the planet extremely dangerous. I understand Warden Olte Signe was injured by this debris. It is almost impossible to avoid. Anyone approaching Retha will have to be very careful from now on.

I would mention that the Navy did carry out a full Navigational Survey of the approaches to Retha not that long ago and I was able to access that report. It makes no reference to rubbish of this kind. In fact it reported that the route was clear of obstructions and that visibility was good. So whatever has caused this has been recent.

Inspector. The next evidence comes from Professor Andemus and is again a recorded report. As I have mentioned Professor Andemus is still on Retha and it is hoped she will be able to give evidence personally on anything further she finds. Have we any further news of her?

Director Erigh Jonsen. I am afraid not. We are becoming concerned.

Professor Andemus. I read about the problems with Retha in the Nature press. I was there once, many years ago and it was quite wonderful. I think mine remains the only sub ocean survey that has been undertaken on the planet. I was very sad to hear things had gone wrong there.

The area of sea on Retha is immense. There is nothing else like it in the Universe. It takes up seventy percent of the planet's surface. It ranges from cold polar oceans to warm tropical seas. Some of these are very shallow and some go down to enormous depths. The breadth of plants and marine life in them rivals anything that can be seen on the land. It is almost impossible to describe the sheer quantities and varieties of the fish and other sea creatures.

For one reason or another, my current planned filming schedule had been cancelled so when I heard of what had happened to Chief Warden Avsa Signe I persuaded my Production Company to fund a filming trip to Retha. Director Jonsen agreed on the understanding that we went at our own risk and that we would make all our findings and material open to this Inquiry and submit a full report.

I went in with a team of four. One camera operator, one sound recordist and two researchers.

At the request of the Directorate we commenced with a shallow depth inspection of one of the coastal areas that Chief Warden Avsa Signe had observed.

We went underwater as soon as we reached Retha and I changed into my normal form.

Private Journal

I tried to see if my system could show videos or stills of all the witnesses. I went into various programmes but got nowhere. Eventually I messaged Peti and she came bustling in minutes later, pressed a few buttons and there was Professor Andemus. I had forgotten how beautiful the Prontteans can be. When flying they are dark, powerful and streamlined and when they swim at depth they are ugly, slimy horrible creatures but when they are in their normal form they are wonderful. Amazing aquamarine fins, goldeny yellow body, silver gills and bright shimmering green underbelly. No wonder her programmes are watched.

COUNCIL of COMMISSIONERS

Retha Inquiry Transcript CONTINUED

Professor Andemus (contd).   We started close to the coast where the water is very shallow. I'm not sure I had been to this exact spot before but if not it wasn't very far from those I had. The water was very disturbed and cloudy which isn't what I remembered. It tasted awful. There were things in it which started making all of us feel ill.   There was also continuous intense sound coming through the water which meant our senses were completely disorientated. This noise never went away. Once it got so loud I could hardly cope. It was bursting my ears. That noise was then followed by an enormous disturbance - big currents of water pushing us everywhere.   I was knocked against rocks and other things I couldn't identify.

The whole atmosphere was horrible.   There were patches of oil. There was debris both on the surface and lying on the sea bed.

My team netted samples of this garbage. We could only collect what we could easily get at so we don't claim it was particularly scientific but it at least gave some indication of what was there. When we examined it later back at the Base we found it was mainly made up of various kinds of manufactured products such as beakers, containers, bags, ropes, bottles and nets. They were predominantly made from an apparently non degradable artificial material and were often coated in oil.

At that point the feeling of sickness became too much for all of us and we swam as quickly as we could away from the coast to where the water was a bit better. There was still continuous noise. It was mainly coming from further away but every now and then something very big would pass above. When that happened the noise was unbearable.

We could still see rubbish floating on the surface above us. At one point there was so much it blocked out the light. It was also lying all over the sea bed, some areas were worse than others. In places there was also evidence that there had been construction or clearance work of some kind. Areas of the sea floor had been completely levelled and there were what we took to be cables and pipes laid across it. In one place large structures had been erected presumably to support things above the water. There were also derelict metal objects, some very large, which had just been abandoned there.

All this wasn't anything like what had been there before. There weren't the vast shoals of fish we saw on our previous visit. There seemed to be less marine vegetation or at least what was there was different. I have never seen damage like it.

I then remembered we had filmed some nearby coral banks the last time. Coral is unusual in these cooler waters and tends to be deeper than the coral reefs you find in tropical seas. We swam around until we found them. I nearly cried. The sea floor looked as if it had been scraped flat. Most of this amazing cold water coral with all its wonderful variety of fish and things like sea anemones, sea urchins, star fish and sea spiders was virtually gone.

Director Erigh Jonsen. After Professor Andemus delivered her report to Base she and her team returned to undertake a deep sea inspection. As I mentioned we have not heard from them since but we will of course notify this Inquiry as soon as we do.

Private Journal

This was getting horrible. When I was on Retha I was sometimes able to see some amazing things when I had my head down under the water feeding - little fish, tiny creatures, plants and coral. At other times, when flying over it, I got views of strange and beautiful creatures swimming on or just under the surface of the sea Funny amphibious creatures with enormous shells, fish that flew, great creatures that would come up and blow water and then disappear again under the surface. Enormous shoals of fish. Why would anything want to destroy all this?

MESSAGE

From: Warden O Signe
To: Chief Warden A Signe

We've had Professor Andemus's evidence. What she found round the coast was pretty bad. She went off to look at the deep oceans but they haven't heard from her since and everyone is getting worried.
I asked you what your Doctors think. **Olte**

From: Chief Warden A Signe
To: Warden O Signe

They don't say much. They can't do much more here and there isn't anything due through for a long time. They are very good. They are now getting me up and making me exercise to help get my other muscles back but they can't do reconstructive surgery which is what I really need.

They are based here permanently serving the Carhynian Archipeligo. The only time they see ships from elsewhere is when they are bringing in an emergency patient so that could happen tomorrow or not for ages. Even then it would only help if they were eventually going to somewhere with larger medical facilities. I suspect I am here for ever. **Da.**

COUNCIL of COMMISSIONERS

Retha Inquiry Transcript CONTINUED

Director Erigh Jonsen. It might be helpful if I summarise where we were by this stage. Chief Warden Avsa Signe and his team had identified that something had caused enormous damage to the Reserve. Professor Andemus' report substantiated this. The photos taken by the Chief Warden and his team and also the Ringooen Navy provided more detail and indicated that the damage appeared to have been caused by a biped species. It could have been more than one species but that looked unlikely. This biped species seemed to have come almost from nowhere in a very short time period. It had not been recorded previously. Its population appeared to be such that it now dominated the planet and needed more and more space to live in. Whether it was an indigenous species or a coloniser or an introduced invasive species we did not know.

Our resources are very limited and, without external funding, we could not easily put together any worthwhile expedition to observe these creatures more closely. Even if we had, the risk to staff would probably have deterred us from doing so. However, we knew that these creatures seemed to be moderately advanced and appeared to have a fairly good grasp of artificial technology. Their forms of transport were evidence of that.

One of the trainee staff who was with us some time ago is now a Principal at the Hundil Communication Centre which most of you will know monitors communications throughout the Universe. On the off chance I contacted her to see if they were intercepting any communications from Retha. She came back to me to ask whether we realised that they were already providing the University of Idreji with links to signal traffic intercepts from Retha.

I immediately contacted the Dean of Idreji and have now received a bundle of submitted research papers, ranging from full Doctorial theses to student essays, based on those intercepted communications. Why they did not think to send us copies before I do not know. It would have saved a lot of time if they had done so. Chief Warden Avsa Signe would probably never have been injured. At the very least we could have given him and his team warning of what to expect. It would also have made our initial work preparing for this Inquiry a lot easier. I have insisted on Assistant Dean Ni Jerp, who I understand supervised this research work and his colleagues, giving evidence. I am grateful to the Inspector for his support on this.

Advokate Otto Slaborg. I object to the inference that my clients have been anything other than totally co-operative.

Inspector. Noted. The next witness is Assistant Dean Ni Jerp.

Assistant Dean Ni Jerp. I am head of the Retha Project at the University of Idreji. We were aware that the Hundil Communication Centre monitors communications throughout the Universe. Sometime ago we notified them, in our role as Administrators of Retha, that if they ever intercepted any communications from Retha we would wish to know. At that time our main interest was to have warning of any intruders.

We heard nothing until very recently when they contacted us to say that they were now picking up significant signal traffic from Retha. They provided us with links and codes and also the language deciphering software, they have developed, to help read this traffic. We gave it initially to our Department of Communications. The volume was enormous – far too big for us to handle. It seemed to be made up of lots of different kinds of communications – individual conversations and messages and what we decided must be public broadcasting. Fortunately Hundill had already been through this process and they suggested that we start by accessing a network they had found which creatures on the planet use for communicating information to each other. Initially our communications people were overwhelmed by all the information it contained. It was rather like accessing an infinite library and the problem was where to look. Eventually we realised that when you got the hang of it you could just ask a question and it would come up with hundreds of what we would call files. This isn't quite as easy as it sounds because the information is of differing quality and it is difficult and time consuming to sift through it. Although Hundill's language deciphering software is impressive it is sometimes difficult to understand everything. However we have now become quite proficient.

When we realised how much information there was we put together the Retha Project team made up mainly of post graduate students but with some assistance from third year undergraduates. The number in the team has varied from time to time. Some have been employed more or less on a permanent basis and some for only temporary periods. It is now our major focus of research on Retha. It can produce enormous amounts of material without the need to be on the ground. Current financial constraints are such that we had not previously been able to do much.

We found that the best way was for each researcher to concentrate on one narrow issue. We don't claim we have found everything yet. Not only is the quantity of information overwhelming, it is also in tens, probably hundreds of different languages. We have currently decided to focus on what seems to be the main language on the planet, or at least the most used, which is the one called English. By concentrating entirely on the information in English it has made it easier to have a consistent approach to working out how and where to best access information, but we cannot claim that it is entirely representative. There may, for instance, be a bias in the information towards the particular socio economic groups who use English rather than those who use one of the other languages but this is unavoidable.

MESSAGE

From: Warden O Signe

To: Chief Warden A Signe

The Director has now introduced some evidence I hadn't heard anything about. It's true, Idreji knew about these creatures all the time. Apparently they've tapped into their communication systems and have had a team of researchers on it. They knew all about this before we went. I've just seen a bit of the detail and it explains who these creatures are and what they are doing. Idreji knew and didn't bother to warn us! No wonder they need a Lawyer. It looks as if they weren't even intending to tell us about it until they were caught out.

Hoagfir – do you remember him?, he will be in the team - says that he's heard that the Director threatened to prosecute Idreji if it didn't get these researchers to give evidence. **Olte**

Assistant Dean Ni Jerp (contd). We have established that the creatures concerned call themselves humans or homo sapiens (thinking creatures). They are mammalian. Although they have differing skin colours and wide ranging physical appearances, they are all the same species, all capable of breeding with each other and producing fertile offspring. They are erect and biped. They can talk. They all have two arms, two legs, two ears through which they hear, two eyes through which they see, a nose through which they breathe and smell and a mouth which they use for talking, eating and also breathing. They are land based. They have limited mobility. They cannot fly, they can only swim limited distances and even then only on the surface not under it. They can walk and run but not at any great speed and only for comparatively short distances. For that reason they mainly live in permanent homes in concentrated areas. They speak a myriad of different languages which seems to depend on where they were born. They cannot control their own body temperature and have to wear clothing. Their flesh burns at, what would be to us, very low temperatures. They mostly have to prepare and cook their food. They do not seem to eat it raw. They can hardly see in the dark.

The reason we can be sure that they are the species responsible for the destruction of the forests and the pollution of the land and sea is that they confirm this in their own communications. In fact they have researched themselves – their origins, development, history, religions and languages as well as their environmental impact on their own planet – in immense detail. We are satisfied that no other species is involved except for some domestic animals which they keep either as pets, beasts of burden or breed for food.

Our first witness is Dr Wenstom Vynack.

Dr Vynack.   I am now a Lecturer in the School of History at the University of Ringooen. I was previously one of the original members of the University of Idreji's Retha Project and I wrote up my research there as part of the Thesis for my Doctorate. My area of research was the origins, development and history of the human species.

As the Assistant Dean has explained we researched this data from the species own electronic record base, which they call the Internet and which is a kind of information exchange. We tapped in questions and then sorted through the hundreds, sometimes thousands of results.

I will summarise as simply as I can what I was able to find out. It is probably not complete but I suspect it is a fairly accurate summary.   For convenience I will use these creatures own time measurements which are Years which is the time taken by Retha to make one revolution around its sun and Days which are based on the rotation of the planet on its axis. All these are very short.

They have traced their very earliest, ape like, ancestors back over **two million years**. Since then they slowly developed to become erect and their brain size expanded considerably. In practical terms what we now know as humans, in something like their present anatomical form, appeared about **two hundred**

thousand years ago by which time they were using basic tools, butchering animals and fishing but were still ape like. Around this time they began to develop language.

Their most noticeable development has been in just the **last ten thousand years**, by which time they were starting to spread and were beginning to change from hunter gatherers to farmers. Most has been in the **last five thousand years**. By then some of them had invented the wheel, were capable of writing in a limited fashion, were wearing clothes and building, in some cases quite large, buildings and structures. They had boats to travel on rivers, lakes and coastal seas.

The development since then was much quicker. Within three thousand years **(two thousand years ago)** they had built cities, with populations in one case of one million, with houses, roads, water supplies, factories and mines. They were making iron tools and were building large fortifications and public buildings.

This was not uniform, some areas advanced quicker than others. Some 'civilisations' went into decline whilst others in completely different parts of the planet emerged and surpassed them. The fact is however, that until **one thousand years ago** the total population of these creatures was only about three hundred million and they had made little serious impact on the environment.

Over the next few hundred years their population expanded significantly. However their technical developments were still comparatively small. The most significant development in that period was the invention, by a couple of tribes or nations of gunpowder which is a primitive explosive. This gave those tribes or nations the power to kill and subdue other humans and also kill most other species. Around **five hundred years ago** they started travelling by sea round the planet in small sailing ships. By then the population was about half a billion and their effect on the planet was starting to become more noticeable. Significant areas of land were being cleared for agriculture and new crops were being cultivated. In some areas this was pronounced but even so spread over the whole planet the effect was still not great.

Then about **two hundred years ago** things changed. That is sometime after the previous official Inspection of Retha by the Conservation Directorate.

The main development was the invention of the steam engine powered by coal or wood. This enabled these humans to make locomotives that run on rails and steam ships that travel on the sea. Instead of journeys taking years they could move large numbers of people and goods considerable distances in days or weeks - which is a measurement of seven of their days. They took people by ship to areas that had previously been barely touched by humans. They constructed railroads across unspoilt plains, prairies and tundra. They killed the vast wild herds that lived there with weapons that used gunpowder. They started clearing and farming the land. They built towns. They dug mines. They cut down the trees for fuel and to build their homes.

Two hundred years ago their population had reached one billion but they had still barely affected half the land mass. Fifty years later **(one hundred and fifty years ago)** because of the steam engine they were everywhere. One of the effects of this was that they introduced, sometimes on purpose, sometimes by accident, alien plants, animals, birds and even illnesses to the places they went to, sometimes with catastrophic consequences.

The discovery and development of electricity came next. That is what has enabled them to develop the technologies they have now – from factories, refineries, oil exploration and mass transport, through to artificial lighting, refrigeration, elevators, electronics, communications and all their thousands and thousands of personal and domestic products.

Shortly after that – a bit over **one hundred years ago** they developed the internal combustion engine and started making small motor vehicles they call cars or automobiles in which they could move around individually and larger ones, called buses, that take more of them and goods vehicles, which they call trucks. They also developed machines with internal combustion engines that can fly. They call these planes or aeroplanes.

Fifty years ago they began to build much larger planes with different engines which hundreds of them could fly in. This meant enormous numbers of these creatures could travel all over the planet in less than a day rather than weeks. Their cities were getting bigger and bigger. They were building everywhere. Their population had reached three and a half billion. To support that number they needed more and more land to live on and to grow crops. They were building machines that could clear vast areas of land and forest in a very short time. The more of them there were, the more they had to clear and destroy.

By far the largest changes have been in just these last fifty years – less than one of their lifetimes. **Fifty years ago** the damage they were causing was manageable. Since then the forests have been reduced by half. Their population has doubled to seven billion. In the same time the population of all other species has halved. This species are now virtually everywhere. The quantity of things they now produce, and apparently need, in comparison to fifty years ago is beyond comprehension. The speed of change and destruction has been something we have never experienced before in the Universe.

Over **the last twenty years** alone their cities have doubled, trebled, and sometimes quadrupled in size. New cities have been built covering vast areas of land. All these need water, food, sewage disposal, power stations, roads, factories, airports and ports. There are factories building things in one part and sending them half way round the planet for sale somewhere else. They have built communities over some of the most beautiful parts of the planet just to go on vacation.

Not much more than **fifty years ago** they were still mainly using natural and recyclable materials. They were making iron and a few other metals but apart from that the materials they were using were mainly natural – clay, stone, wood, straw, wool, leather, feathers, silk and cotton. They are now dependant on artificial materials.

Everything they do needs more and more energy. They now use not only wood and coal for fuel but also oil, gas and nuclear. The more of them there are the more they have to take from the planet. Their population is still increasing. On their own estimations it will get to eleven billion in the next fifty years.

Inspector. Thank you Dr Vynack. Are there any questions?

Advokate Otto Slaborg. So there is no misunderstanding are you confirming that this species definitely wasn't introduced and that there is no doubt it is an indigenous species?

Dr Vynack. Yes.

Advokate Otto Slaborg. In your opinion did the University of Idreji have any role in assisting its development?

Dr Vynack. That was never discussed or suggested by anyone whilst I was part of the programme.

Advokate Otto Slaborg. Do you think the University of Idreji should have done more to stop this damage happening?

Dr Vynack. I wasn't part of the Administration Team. That was entirely separate. My role was purely research.

MESSAGE

From: Warden O Signe

To: Chief Warden A Signe

They say these creatures have devolved from hairy ape like creatures. Can you remember anything like that around when we ran it? By the way the Director asks whether you want to give evidence? **Olte.**

From: Chief Warden A Signe

To: Warden O Signe

We did come across hairy bipeds from time to time, they were mainly hiding in the forests so we couldn't get a good look at them. There were various types but I'm not sure we were ever able to properly distinguish one from another. I assume these creatures must have been one of those. I don't think there is much point in me giving evidence. I'm not sure I can add anything to what you've told them. **Da**

Assistant Dean Ni Jerp.   Our next witness is Research Fellow Olwen Slliga MSc.

Olwen Slliga.   I am now a Junior Research Fellow in the School of Developmental Science at the University of Pointer.   Previously I was a supervising Researcher on the University of Idreji's Retha Project. My own research was into the technical development of this species.

Physically they are fairly primitive. Apart from the fact they can stand on their two hind legs, which means that their forehands are free to do and make things, they are comparatively immobile.

As Assistant Dean Ni Jerp has said they cannot fly. They cannot swim far and then only on the surface, not below it. They can walk and run short distances but not very fast.   Their control of their body temperature is limited so they have to wear clothes and, depending on where they live, heat their homes.

There are many, many species of bird, fish and animal on Retha that are physically far more advanced. Take for example a bird that can fly from one end of the planet to the other or the turtles that can swim across oceans or mice that can collapse their skeletons to get through very small holes.

The only advantage this species has are large brains, the ability to speak and communicate with each other and being able to make tools - because their arms are free they have been able to develop hands and fingers. As Dr Vynack has told you, their technical developments were slow until only about two hundred years ago. Until then they were probably still in balance with nature.

Since then they have built tools and machines that enable them to compensate for their physical limitations and to dominate the planet. They have the ability to kill anything they want, including themselves. They can clear vast areas of land with machines. They can drill for oil even in deep water or in the polar areas.

Well over half of them are now urban dwellers. The rest still live in rural communities but mainly to produce crops and goods for those who live in the urban areas. There are still a few 'primitive' communities that are virtually untouched by the 'civilisation' around them, but not many.

Because they have invented motor vehicles they can now move around in a way they couldn't even a hundred years ago. Previous to that they had to live within walking distance of where they worked or farmed. They don't have to grow or collect their own food, this is done for them on vast farms sometimes on the other side of the planet. They purchase what they need from outlets in their cities.

These urban or city areas vary a lot. The difference can be staggering. There are those with modern buildings and advanced infrastructure – roads, transport systems, sewers, water, electricity and large shopping areas selling anything you can think of. Here there is a high standard of living. There are others where the buildings are no more than shacks, where there are no paved streets or sewers or running water. Here several people will live in one room and there can be real poverty. In some places the two can be found in the same city where there are advanced infrastructures in one part and slums in another.

All these cities depend on food and water coming in from outside. As they have expanded, more land has had to be cleared elsewhere to feed them. Their fuel - wood, coal, oil and gas also has to be brought in.

They spend their lives in these vast sprawls of buildings never seeing countryside. In some areas there are only a few trees left dotted here and there. They have completely destroyed the natural environment. They have pushed out or killed most other creatures. They have constructed their own private worlds. They are not bothered with what was there before.

The real problem they have with their cities, is that they are already at breaking point. Their infrastructure – water, sewerage, electricity, roads and transport – are overstretched and can't cope with yet more growth. The older properties are rundown and beginning to become slums. There aren't the resources to replace them. They just keep patching things but they can't keep up, except in the very rich areas.

The intense city life is fine for many – particularly the better off – but for the poor and not so bright and the elderly or disabled it's horrible. Because of their limited mobility these creatures have developed motor vehicles to enable them to travel. There are now so many that they dominate the cities. They have had to build larger and larger highways but those only make it worse for those of them who don't have vehicles, particularly the elderly.

I can't imagine how stressful living in those conditions must be. The level of crime is far beyond anything we could envisage.

Advokate Otto Slaborg. Do you agree that it would have been impossible for the University's Administration

Team to detect this development let alone do anything about it bearing in mind the very short timescale it has happened over?

Olwen Slliga.   No. I am not sure I agree. Isn't that what a Ranger Team was supposed to be there for?

Private Journal

This was getting so horrible I couldn't go on. I tried doing other things. I went through various files waiting on my desk but I couldn't concentrate. I wandered into my private quarters and tried to do domestic tasks but it didn't do any good.

Retha was the most wonderful time of my life. Nothing before or after even started to come up to it. I may have acquired high position and influence and I suppose power but the wonder of Retha far surpasses that.

It wasn't just Avsa. It was also that amazing place, that perfect paradise. I knew nasty things happened, one group of animals attacking, bringing down and eating more vulnerable ones. Big fish eating little fish. But at the end of it there was a balance which no species, even the biggest, could change. All these billions of creatures of millions of different kinds all living together but free to develop in their own way. The very basis of evolution may seem brutal – the survival of the fittest, but the reality is that, provided there is a balance of nature, species are able to coexist and evolve. They had been doing so on Retha for millions of years and we were there to make sure it continued.

It never occurred to us that the risk would come from within. To us the threat was always from outside – poachers, tourists, colonisers. That is why I had still thought that this must be the result of outside intervention. It was almost sacrilege to think that one of Retha's creatures could do this to their own world.

COUNCIL of COMMISSIONERS

Retha Inquiry Transcript CONTINUED

Assistant Dean Ni Jerp. The next witness is Dr Ryw Kryg.

Dr Ryw Kryg. I was the Senior Researcher on the Retha Project at the University of Idreji under Assistant Dean Ni Jerp. I am now a Fellow of the Institute for Environmental Protection.

I am an Environmental Biochemist. My particular research on Retha was focussed on the pollution caused by this species.

The fact that I was able to dedicate a Doctorate Thesis to that one subject speaks for itself.

In my full report I have listed all the individual sources of pollution I found, so I will just summarise the most significant ones here. One of the biggest single causes is their cities. Hundreds of thousands, sometimes millions of these creatures all living together in one place. They have changed from an agrarian society to an industrialised one in a very short time.

There are now factories, mines and power stations virtually everywhere all spewing out pollution of one kind or another. Their agriculture is now so industrialised - in order to serve the cities - that it is in itself another major cause of pollution. Their cars and trucks and planes and all their other machinery add to all this pollution.

Perhaps the most horrifying is these creatures own domestic sewage. There will always be nasty things in sewage, particularly untreated sewage. That is inevitable. In their case germs like gastroenteritis, E.coli, hepatitis, typhoid, paratyphoid and cholera and things like parasitic worms. When there were fewer of them and they ingested natural foods the ecosystems could manage. The problem they now have is the sheer quantity they are producing and the effect it is having on the environment. They have had to develop very complex toilet and sewage systems – far more complex than anything I've come across in the rest of the Cosmos – but then we don't have these enormous concentrations of population. Many cities still just dump it in the rivers and the sea. Some do try to treat it but even then the 'treated' liquids and solids still have to go somewhere. Whether they discharge this sewage into rivers or into the sea or bury it or treat it or 'compost' it, much of it will end up one way or the other back in their own water supplies and food chain.

They have for instance found significant concentrations of human female oestrogen hormonal compounds in their rivers and coastal waters. The quantity is so great that there is evidence that these hormones are having a feminising effect on male fish. That gives you some idea of the numbers of these creatures.

It gets worse. They are now also using quantities of artificial products in their homes such as detergents, chemicals and toiletries all of which also end up in the sewage systems. They are also ingesting more and more artificial substances such as medicines and food additives. Some of these will break down but most won't. Then there are all the toilet and sanitary products these creatures apparently need, which they put down their sewers and drains – apparently without a thought. Where do they think it all goes to?

If it doesn't sound too dramatic they are beginning to become smothered by their own pollution.

Private Journal

It would have been wonderful even if we had met in the middle of the Klangiten desert (which is as desolate as you get!), but to have the first and I suppose last love affair of my life in somewhere as idyllic as Retha was something no-one could deserve. My ancestors must have been looking kindly on me.

When we started Avsa's behaviour was absolutely correct. He made a point of keeping a respectable distance. If I moved too close he would move away. Then one day, I think it was probably seven or eight days after we'd set out, he was pointing something out to me and he touched my body so I could see where he was looking.

After that we were like infatuated children. We never wanted to separate. It was as if we were glued to each other.

We would fly together, I'd lay one of my wings on his and we'd each use our other wing to fly as if we were one. We took a long time to get the hang of it. It wasn't comfortable to begin with, it isn't normal to move only one wing. It is very difficult to learn to stop moving the other. We kept falling out of the sky until we got used to it. It was wonderful!

To see as much as possible we flew most of the day only dropping down in early evening to feed and make love. I was a virgin of course. I don't know whether Avsa was. I assumed so. He was wonderful and gentle. We would then sleep where we were. I never felt afraid even though there were very hostile large animals in some places as well as things like snakes.

Our size helped but looking back I realise Avsa knew the safe places. Some areas, particularly islands, had few if any things that could harm us.

From then on we didn't have a care. We spent the whole of the time just flying around looking at things each more beautiful than the next. We spent several wonderful days over vast expanses of tropical coral reefs. The sea was so clear you could see deep down a myriad of coloured creatures. I never tired of looking at the coral - infinite numbers of tiny tiny creatures all working together to produce a natural unspoilt masterpiece.

We flew from there across a vast expanse of empty ocean. Just the odd tiny island dotted around in a deep blue sea. We would see one we really liked and would come back to it in the evening to feed, make love and sleep.

Once or twice we received weak messages from the Director enquiring somewhat anxiously where we were and were we alright. I replied we were fine and would return soon.

Then we just went on round and round, criss-crossing where we had been a few days before or a few days before that but always seeing something different, something we'd missed.

Never before or after, have I felt so free of responsibilities. My whole life since has been about doing what is required of me.

Dr Ryw Kryg (contd). I suppose the form of pollution these creatures produce which I find most wanton is the manufacture and disposal of plastics. Plastics are an artificial material made from hydrocarbons derived from oil they extract from the ground. The process of drilling and extracting oil, in itself, causes significant damage to the environment. Particularly if there are spillages either in the drilling or production process or in transporting it to where it is needed. There are now oil and gas rigs all over the planet not just on land but also on the sea. Some are in what were the last of the unspoilt areas. Any spillage, particularly at sea, causes immediate damage to birds, fish and marine life and long term damage to the sea bed.

These creatures use plastics for making the things they need because they are easier to produce than natural products. They use them in virtually everything - clothing, packaging, bottles, bags, containers, furnishing, machinery and building - you could go on listing them forever.   The problem is that plastics are virtually indestructible.   Some will degrade but most will be around for hundreds of years.

A lot of the plastic rubbish eventually ends up in the sea. This is what Professor Andemus saw. Some is dumped there, some is blown or swept out there and some is thrown off ships. This has, over a very short period, created vast floating masses of waste plastic made up of things like bottles, bags, cups and containers.   These creatures produce between five hundred billion and one trillion plastic bags every year. They manufacture fifty billion plastic bottles each year. They use them once and throw them away. There is an area they themselves call the 'Great Pacific Garbage Patch' in the sea off somewhere they know as California. It is probably the largest rubbish site in the Universe but there are others on Retha almost as large.

The individual items of plastic in the sea are now believed to outnumber sealife. Millions of birds and marine animals are killed by it. The plastic suffocates them, strangles and injures them. What is worse they swallow the smaller pieces, which either poisons them or stays in their stomachs and makes it difficult for them to eat. Some of the most unpleasant are the very small plastic particles, called micro beads, which these creatures put in cosmetics to make themselves beautiful. When they wash them off they go into the drains and then out to the sea and into the stomachs of anything out there.

They estimate it will take between five hundred to one thousand years for most plastic to degrade but they honestly don't know.

To mention a couple of other areas. Warden Signe referred to debris around the rim of the planet. This species started putting things into space about fifty years ago. Initially those were elementary satellites or capsules for research purposes but later they have been for communications. These have just been left up there even when they become obsolete. Some have broken up, some have damaged each other, some have been partially destroyed on re-entry. The result is an unpleasant ribbon of lethal rubbish all round the edge of the planet. According to their own figures there are now hundreds of thousands of bits of debris out there. Some may be very small but some are large. Together they weigh over two thousand tons and it's increasing all the time.

Another major source of pollution is radioactivity. They learnt the technology to divide atoms about seventy years ago and have used the power to produce electricity and for weapons. They now have redundant nuclear power stations and vast dumps of radioactive waste which they don't know what to do with. The discharges, accidental and otherwise, from these dumps, from weapons testing and from the nuclear plants themselves, has meant that there is radioactive contamination over the whole planet, particularly the seas.

The fact is the list of the waste they are dumping into their own environment is endless – domestic, industrial, manufacturing and agricultural. Most is either burnt, which causes air pollution or buried in enormous rubbish dumps or dumped in the rivers or seas. Lots are just left lying around spoiling and polluting the planet for ever. They are a wasteful, untidy species. There are abandoned derelict buildings, old mines, factories, railways, rusting machinery and vehicles everywhere. There are also the leftovers from their many wars. There are vast areas where it isn't safe to go because of unexploded bombs and mines. They have even dumped these in the sea. There is hardly anywhere they haven't spoilt.

Although I could list more and more of the types of pollution this species produces the primary cause is simply their cities. As their population increases more and more of these creatures have to live in them. These cities are entirely artificial, nothing is natural. Everything has to be brought in. They are having to constantly expand to cope with the increasing population – more buildings needing more roads, sewers, transport systems and utilities. All these need concrete, which I haven't mentioned. When there were less of them they used stone and clay for building which were natural. Now because they need so much more they are reliant on concrete which requires vast amounts of energy to produce.

They are constantly squeezing more and more people in to these cities. Where there is still any open space left they build on it. I don't know how long they think they can carry on like this.

I could go on for ever but I suspect I've made the point. I don't think I've even mentioned all the horrific stuff they spew out of their mines and factories but it's all in my report. If this species has done this amount of damage in just fifty years, it is frightening to think what damage they'll cause in the next fifty.

Advokate Otto Slaborg.   In your opinion did the University of Idreji have any role in assisting the development of this species.

Dr Ryw Kryg.   That was never discussed or suggested by anyone whilst I was part of the project.

President Henk O Kang.   Do you think the University of Idreji should have done more to stop this damage happening?

Dr Ryw Kryg.   Yes I do. I passed my findings to my Head of Department but heard nothing more.

Private Journal

I heard from Peti.

"I've made enquiries about getting Chief Warden Avsa Signe to a bigger hospital. He can't fly himself and the hospital ship he's on is based where it is permanently and there are no plans to move it. No other ships are scheduled for a long time but if one comes they'll put him on it. I've asked but we don't have anything suitable available. Do you want me to see if any of the Members have something nearby we could borrow? I am sure they'd help if they knew it was for you."

I replied telling her to leave contacting any of the Members for the moment. I asked her instead whether it was feasible for me to go there, how long it takes nowadays and when I would have the time to spare.

Inspector. Our next witness is Hanna Langed.

Hanna Langed. I graduated in Agricultural Science at the University of Idreji. Whilst I was there I was seconded to the Retha project for one semester. The idea was that it would help me to study other agricultural systems.

I went through an induction process which enabled me to access the Retha communication network, after that I was left on my own. I submitted a dissertation at the end of my secondment and I have continued to study Retha since and hope to be able to make it the subject of my PhD thesis. I am now working under Dr Ryw Kryg and she suggested that I gave evidence.

My study was split into three parts – what are they growing, how they are growing it and why they are growing it. The first two are pretty obvious. It was only after I had been doing my research for a while that I began to ask why they are growing some of these things.

Most other 'civilisations' in the known Cosmos, because of their low populations, have low intensity agriculture which has little impact on the environment. Retha is totally different, it is now geared to produce as much as possible as intensively as possible for the benefit of one species. You have already heard of the clearance of the forests and other wild areas. You have seen the photos of the extent that these areas have been cleared. They have cut down around ninety percent of the forests in the temperate zone. The figure for the rainforests is around fifty percent but this is probably only because they are more remote. One source estimates that even these are now being cut down at the rate of thirty million acres every year.

The loss of all these habitats, to make room for more cities and to grow more crops together with the indiscriminate use of herbicides and insecticides, is the prime reason for the drop in the insect, bird and mammal population.

They have over a very short period developed a range of insecticides to kill anything that eats their crops. Some are really unpleasant like organochlorides, organophosphates and polychlorinated biphenyls all of which would be illegal in the rest of the Cosmos. The damage they do indiscriminately to small insect life is unimaginable but they are also toxic to virtually any living creature. The problem, because of the quantities they are using them in, is that they are now everywhere in the food chain and water courses. They now affect virtually all creatures including these humans themselves.

What I would like to explain is what this species are growing and the methods they use. Over the last two hundred years they have cleared more and more land for intensive agriculture. They have become very proficient at producing as much as they can. They have vast areas each growing just one single crop. They have machines designed simply to sow, cultivate and harvest that crop. They use huge amounts of artificial fertilisers and pesticides to increase yields. They have had to build irrigation systems to provide water for these crops. They have even genetically modified them both to increase yield and reduce threats from plant disease. Whilst all this may be producing more food, it has caused enormous damage to the environment and the other indigenous species both fauna and flora.

These single crops are mainly basic items such as wheat, corn and rice. It depends on where they are. There are others such as cassava, soya bean, millet, pulses, fruit and vegetables. As this species has become more prosperous the demand for additional crops has increased. Many are now grown in one country and flown half way round the planet whilst they are still fresh.

They have also increased their taste for eating other animals. A lot of the land that has been cleared is used for intensive meat production – particularly beef.

The strange thing is that over the last ten years or so they have diverted a lot of land to the production of crops used to make fuels. In other words instead of eating these crops they are processing them into things like ethanol for use in power generation and in vehicles and planes. They produce ethanol fuel from sugar and palm oil. They are doing the same with corn. They seem to think this is better for the environment. In actual fact by diverting crops and land from food production they have increased food prices and created shortages amongst the poorer human inhabitants of the planet. More significantly it has meant that even more forest and natural areas have been cleared to make room for these crops.

Inspector. Thank you. Advokate Slaborg, I assume you have questions.

Advokate Otto Slaborg. Thank you Inspector, I think I have already made my point.

Inspector. Our next witness is Olegl Raphidor.

Olegl Raphidor.   Thank you.   I am a third year biological science student at the University of Idreji.   In the semester just gone I was placed with the Retha Project.   One of my essays was on the animals that have been brought to extinction or near extinction by Homo Sapiens.   There were so many examples I just chose those which I thought were the worst.

Two hundred years ago there were estimated to be thirty million bison in the great plains and prairies of the mid west of what this species calls North America.   At that time those plains had hardly been settled by humans.   The few that were there were indigenous nomadic tribes who killed just the number of bison they needed to feed and clothe themselves.

Then two hundred years ago other humans started coming, slowly at first but then in very large numbers - particularly after the invention of steamships and railroads.   They had guns which the indigenous people didn't.   They started to kill the buffalo on an industrial scale.   Some for their hides, some for their meat and some just because they were a threat to their crops.   By one hundred years ago possibly as few as one thousand buffalo remained.   Around thirty million had been killed, most of them in a forty year period!

Another horrible example is deep sea fishing.   This is still going on.   This species has fished the seas ever since they first evolved.   Until about one hundred years ago this was mainly done locally and was in balance with nature.   Now, mainly because of the introduction of much larger trawlers, they have been able to fish on a scale it is difficult to imagine.

The trawlers they have now can find shoals of fish electronically.   They can fish far offshore in deep water. The fish they catch are processed and packed on board.

These are bottom trawlers which drag giant weighted nets at depths of two kilometres or more along the ocean floor far out at sea, scooping up whatever is there. This means they catch and destroy not just fish but seals and dolphins and also everything there is on the sea bed - like ancient coral, anemones and fields of sea sponge. They are laying waste to huge areas of the sea floor. They haul up all the fish they catch but any unwanted or undersize fish are just thrown away dead or dying.

These humans own figures show that they are now catching the fish faster than they can reproduce. One calculation is that if they go on like this there will be hardly any fish left in thirty years from now. This will not only affect the other marine species that rely on fish for food but also those humans, who live next to the sea, for whom fish is the staple diet. Some of those will be the poorest on the planet. There are reports that many local fishing communities all over the planet are already suffering from this over fishing.

One of the symptoms of over fishing is the drop in the seabird population. This is estimated to have gone down from three hundred million birds sixty years ago to seventy million today. That is partly as a result of over fishing and partly due to human pollution. This compares with human population which has more than doubled to seven billion in the same period.

The last example I chose was elephants. These are wonderful great lumbering animals with huge bodies and long noses. They are the largest land animals on Retha and are amongst the most intelligent. Their brains are similar in complexity to humans but larger. They have survived in their natural habitats for fifty million years. Some particular species of them have enormous tusks. One hundred years ago there were more than three million of that species according to the humans own figures. Now there are less than five hundred thousand and they are being killed by these humans at the rate of around thirty thousand a year just so their tusks can be turned into ivory ornaments.

Advokate Otto Slaborg. I have no questions.

MESSAGE

From: Warden O Signe
To: Chief Warden A Signe

Idreji's Researchers are coming up with loads of stuff about these creatures. There isn't any doubt who they are but I think Idreji have made more of their Project than it really was. I don't think it was really anything to do with the Administration of Retha. Some of it is very good but some are not much more than student essays. Most of them were third year or post grad students like the ones we used to get. The Assistant Dean knew his stuff but I don't think he did any of the research. We all want to know why Idreji didn't do anything if they knew this much. Why didn't they tell us as soon as they realised what they'd got? Did they help these humans do you think? Director Jonsen isn't asking them any questions. Hoagfir thinks that he did a deal with Idreji that in return for all this stuff he'd go easy on them. **Olte**

From: Chief Warden A Signe
To: Warden O Signe

I can't believe Idreji really would have interfered by helping one particular species. It is against everything we stand for. Even so the time scales are very suspicious. One moment this species wasn't there, the next they are crawling all over the planet. With a bit of luck Henk Kang of UWPF will raise this. He was really brassed off when Idreji got the contract. In fairness to Idreji, the time from first knowing about these creatures' communications system to now has been very short. I'm not sure they could have acted much quicker.

How is Hoagfir? Give him my greetings. Who else have you got on the team? **Da**

COUNCIL of COMMISSIONERS

Retha Inquiry Transcript CONTINUED

Inspector. Our next witness is Atil Ontahkus.

Atil Ontahkus. I graduated in Marine Biology at the University of Idreji. In my final year I was placed with the Retha Project for one semester to research the practical effects of human pollution on marine life and this formed part of my final year course work.

Eighty percent of marine debris is now plastic. This has happened in less than sixty years. Old fishing nets made of plastic are left or lost in the ocean and entangle fish, dolphins, sea turtles, sharks, sea birds, crabs and a host of other creatures. These may simply stop them from swimming or it may suffocate them or prevent them from eating or just drown them. Vast numbers die every year as a result.

Many sea creatures consume plastic waste by mistake because it often looks like their natural food. For example Turtles eat plastic bags because they look like jelly fish. This gets stuck in their throats and prevents them from eating. Six pack rings from drinks cans get stuck round sea birds beaks so they can't eat.

Although plastics do not easily biodegrade they do disintegrate into smaller and smaller pieces which are absorbed by many sea creatures either from sea water itself or from eating other creatures. Plastic contaminates have now been found in the stomach of most marine birds and animals to the extent that they may have difficulty digesting food.

Other witnesses have already mentioned the volumes of excrement that these creatures discharge into the sea from their cities. By chance I came across an article on their Internet about the sewage discharges from ships. Many of these humans, particularly from the richer countries now go on holiday on 'Cruise Ships' which can take thousands of them. Although there are some rules many of these ships just dump their sewage and waste water into the sea where they are. Think of what the effect that amount of human waste, and everything else that's with it, must have on the marine life in that area.

Another thing I found was that these creatures move things round on ships in big metal containers. Thousands of them are washed off into the sea each year. Some sink and litter the bottom of the sea. Some carry on floating on the surface. Some break open so their contents fall out and add to all the other rubbish floating around.

I was only a third year student and to be honest this was just a piece of course work but I was disgusted that any apparently intelligent species could allow all this to happen.

Inspector. Are there any questions for this witness?

Advokate Otto Slaborg. I have no questions.

Inspector. I now call Awosyre Pahmbach who is appearing at his own request.

Advokate Otto Slaborg. Sir I strongly object to this witness. We do not regard his evidence as objective or credible. He has made wild and totally unsubstantiated allegations about Idreji's administration of the Reserve. As a result my clients had no alternative but to terminate his engagement.

Inspector. With respect Advokate Slaborg it is for me to decide whether Mr Pahmbach's evidence is credible and I can hardly do that until I've heard it.

Awosyre Pahmbach MSc. Thank you Sir. I was a Researcher with the Idreji Retha Project for one and a half semesters, until my appointment was summarily terminated. I have a Masters Degree in Biological Sciences from the University of Pointer and had been accepted as a PhD student in the Centre for Evolutionary Studies at Idreji.

I specifically applied to Idreji because of their reputation in Evolutionary Science. They only have two or three PhD opportunities each year in that Department and I was lucky to get one.

It was suggested when I got there that I should do my thesis on the evolution of Homo Sapiens on Retha, as part of their Retha Project.

I was provided with access to these humans' communication systems and shown how to use it.

Although strictly I was attached to the Centre for Evolutionary Studies I was actually based at the Retha Project. At that time the main topic of debate was how a species could come from apparently nothing to where it is now in just ten thousand of their years which is less than some of our lifetimes.

The question was were they indigenous or were they introduced and did they have external assistance in their development say in the form of education or training?

It didn't take long to establish, from all the evidence you have already heard, that they are indigenous and that their physical development over at least two million years was as the result of natural evolution. Even so I had intended with the benefit of all the evidence available, to write the first half of my thesis on that. If nothing else it would put that issue to bed.

As to whether they received any external assistance, my appointment was terminated before I could get very far, so I had only initiated very preliminary research.

Private Journal

I couldn't get my head round the time scales. Ten thousand years sounded a long time ago but how long was it after I was there? We surely couldn't have missed all this in our journeys round the planet. Even if we weren't studying things as closely as we might we went everywhere, probably several times. I certainly couldn't remember seeing these creatures but then we saw thousands of animals of all different kinds and I wouldn't remember all of them. If they were there, there can't have been many of them. I tried to work this out using the time convertor they had provided. I eventually got it to work. Ten thousand years was long after Avsa and I were flying untroubled round Retha.

Awosyre Pahmbach (cont). The advance and spread of this species has been phenomenal. If you were looking at it in sporting terms it took them two million years to do the first lap, five thousand years to do the second and only another five thousand to do the remaining eight. That is why, inevitably, questions will be asked as to whether this could have happened naturally or whether they had outside assistance around five or ten thousand years ago.

I raised this in one of my essays merely as a point of interest and a possible explanation for the speed in which this species has developed. The problem, which I suppose I should have realised, is that the University of Idreji was the Administrator of the Reserve throughout the time in question and controlled access to it. If it turned out there was any basis for my concerns it suggested that Idreji might have been a party to it or at least knew about it.

I suppose the reason this did not occur to me was that our project was entirely separate from the Administration of Retha and we regarded all this simply as an interesting academic research project. We weren't concerned at the practicalities.

Immediately my essay was seen I was called to see Assistant Dean Ni Jerp and was summarily dismissed.

Inspector. Thank you Mr Pahmbach. I think we have questions for you from both Advokate Slaberg and President Henk O Kang of the UWPF.

Advokate Otto Slaborg. Have you any evidence at all that the University of Idreji assisted this species' education, training or development?

Awosyre Pahmbach. No.

Advokate Otto Slaborg. Are you suggesting the University of Idreji should have done more to stop this damage happening?

Awosyre Pahmbach. I wasn't part of the Administration Team. That was entirely separate. My role was purely research.

Advokate Otto Slaborg. The fact is that despite the wild accusations you have made your knowledge of Evolution is very limited is it not. You just have a Master's Degree in Biology. Is that correct?

Awosyre Pahmbach. Yes.

Advokate Otto Slaborg. You have no qualifications at all in Evolution. Is that correct?

Awosyre Pahmbach. Yes.

Advokate Otto Slaborg. I put it to you that you are totally unqualified to make the comments you have.

Awosyre Pahmbach. I have only said what I thought. I was good enough for the University to accept me as a PhD Student.

Advokate Otto Slaborg. I have no further questions.

President Henk O Kang. In your opinion was this species assisted in its development?

Awosyre Pahmbach. We really have no evidence that it was. Only niggling doubts. If it was, it was done in localised areas which might explain why one locality developed quicker than others.

President Henk O Kang. Is it true to say that all this species' most significant developments happened since the University of Idreji took over the Administration of Retha?

Awosyre Pahmbach. Yes I suppose it is.

President Henk O Kang. Who was Professor Tinn?

Awosyre Pahmbach. He was the foremost Evolutionary Scientist of his time. It was as a result of his work that Idreji established itself as the leading centre for Evolutionary Studies.

President Henk O Kang. Was he the University of Idreji's first Administrator of Retha?

Ewosyre Pahmbach. Yes

Advokate Otto Slaborg. Really I must protest. What is that question intended to imply?

President Henk O Kang. I merely record that the development of this species particularly in writings, religions and building started after Idreji took over the Administration and Professor Tinn became the Administrator.

Advokate Otto Slaborg. That is outrageous. You are making grave and totally unsubstantiated allegations against a great scientist who cannot defend himself.

Inspector. Gentlemen, I think that is enough.

Assistant Dean Ni Jerp. If I may interject here. To be scientifically correct, the time we are talking about also coincides with the ending of a significant ice age which affected a large area of what is now the temperate part of Retha. Once the ice receded these humans, and indeed other species, were able to expand and develop into new, perhaps more fertile areas. That is another and perhaps more likely explanation for this apparent leap in their development.

Awosyre Pahmbach. If I can come back for a moment. My question would not be whether this species was assisted but whether the whole planet was assisted. The species we are talking about is in many ways pretty unexceptional. But how can anyone explain how something as wonderful and varied as this planet could just happen. It is like an enormous garden. There are millions of birds, fish, mammals, reptiles, insects, plants and trees all different, all fitting together. All doing incredible things. However did that happen? Can we really dismiss the idea that at one point long, long ago there was a gardener? In the past such thoughts were dismissed as unscientific but increasingly we are not sure we can provide all the answers.

Inspector. Our last witness is Dr Thawlying Thernjie.

Thawlying Thernjie. I was a member of Idreji University's Retha Project when I was doing research for my MSc. I am an Anthropologist and my interest was in these human's culture and beliefs. I was not asked by the University to give evidence. I only discovered about this Inquiry by chance.

Over their recent history these humans have developed strong, sometimes very militant, religious beliefs. Although there are now half a dozen main religions there are hundreds more, all of which believe something different. They are mainly distributed geographically. Most religions seem to believe in a God. Sometimes more than one. These religions have developed comparatively recently – over say the last five thousand years.

Although they have different beliefs there is one constant theme throughout most of them and that is that the human race is the 'ordained' species and the planet is theirs. Many of their religions teach this. They have been brought up to believe that "God made man in his own image" and that they are the "Children of God" and that God gave them, as one of their religious books says, "Dominion over the fish of the sea and over the fowl of the air and over every living thing that moveth upon the planet".

If you think about it that excuses everything they've done.

They genuinely believe they are the only species that matters. If a dog, or bear or a lion kills a man they kill it because it is 'dangerous'. If a man kills a dog or a bear or a lion that's allowed.

They really believe they have the right to do whatever they want. They don't consider any of the other species. They are ignorant of the balance of nature, that every creature and every plant is inter-dependent. They don't worry that crops only get fertilised because of bees and other insects and that they are killing them with insecticides, nor that if they carry on stripping the seas there will be no fish. They just aren't interested. If they want to clear land or forest they can, they don't give any thought to the thousands of other species that live there.

Whether they are still religious or not, and many aren't, virtually every human instinctively believes that the planet is there for them and they have the right to do whatever they like with it. They really think that everything, the land itself and all the birds, animals, plants and trees on it, belongs to them. They fence 'their' land off so wild animals cannot move safely from and to their traditional feeding and breeding grounds. They build roads across them so millions of animals are killed every year. They erect pylons and cables and wind turbines that birds fly into. It doesn't occur to them that all the other animals, birds and other creatures have been on the planet much longer than them and have just as great a right to it.

S

Private Journal

Avsa and I used to talk about how Retha was created. We could not believe that it could have just developed naturally. That something as wonderful as this could happen by accident.

The usual questions came up. If something from outside had created it who were they and who created them? Avsa obviously had no idea then who I was. I assumed he realised I was from some important background but not more than that.

Natural evolution is so much part of our beliefs that I and my Sisters do not dwell too much on the question of how even we came to be here in the first place.

To us the natural change and development of species is just normal and desirable. Even in my lifetime I have seen species develop amazingly. Travel as we do it today is an example. We are no longer the only ones who can move freely through the Universe. It has been interesting to see how different species have developed distinct means of star travel. When I went to Retha originally it was a life time posting for most non-cygne species. It took so long for them to get there, that there was no real prospect of them ever going home. It was rather like the early human travellers Dr Vynack referred to. Looking at the photo list of the witnesses, I could see several species who still rely on life suspension but at least one was a Mnglisk who are now beginning to evolve the ability to manipulate time. I remember we discussed it at a conference a while ago and two Mnglisks came to explain what they could do and how the ability had developed, which was quite accidental.

As to the rest of the witnesses they were mainly Idrejians, who have longish life spans, but only limited space travel ability which is why they would only have wanted to administer Retha. The rest were super energy travellers like ourselves and Professor Andemus and her other Prontteans.

Inspector. Thank you Mr Thernjie.

As you know the purpose of this Second Section of this Inquiry is to establish the issues which seem to boil down to whether there has been excessive and unjustified damage to this Protected Reserve and if so who is responsible. I do not think there are any more witnesses. If that is correct I would now ask any interested parties who wish to do so to make final submissions on those limited questions.

As to what steps should be taken, if it is established there has been excessive and unjustified damage, is for Section Three.

Advokate Slaborg, do you wish to make a submission?

Advokate Otto Slaborg. Thank you Inspector. My Clients have reviewed all the evidence and accompanying reports and papers that have been presented to this Inquiry. I am instructed to say the University of Idreji agrees that extensive, unjustifiable and unacceptable damage has been caused to the Reserve and that there is no doubt that the species called Homo Sapiens is responsible.

Inspector. Thank you. Director do you wish to comment?

Director Erigh Jonsen. In our view there is no doubt that extensive, unjustifiable and possibly irreversible, damage has been caused to the Reserve. We agree on the basis of all we have heard and all the background papers that there can be no doubt that Homo Sapiens is at least primarily responsible.

Inspector.   Does any one else wish to make any submissions on this point?

President Henk O Kang.   I can only agree with what has been said.   There can be no doubt of the horrific extent of the damage and who is responsible.   I remain of the view that we should also know how this has happened and why it wasn't detected earlier.   I am concerned that if we just go on now to discuss remedies, we will not learn the lessons of this sorry affair.

Advokate Otto Slaborg.   As I have said previously my Clients would strongly object to any suggestion that there is any culpability on their part.   I do not think anything would be gained by wasting time on what could have happened.   We are where we are.   The only function of this Inquiry must be to identify what we can best do to remedy the situation.

Inspector.   Is there anyone else who wishes to comment?   In particular does anyone disagree?

No?

In that case and in view of what has been said, with which I totally concur, I find that excessive and unjustified damage has been illegally caused to the Retha Protected Reserve and that the species called Homo Sapiens is wholly or mainly responsible.

As to the points raised by President Henk O Kang I agree with him that the lessons of this affair need to be learned and I intend to make recommendations in my report. I would ask that you address me on those points after we have completed Section Three.

Turning to Section Three. Before we consider the possible Remedies I would like to clarify a few issues. I propose to ask a number of specific questions and would invite any interested parties to comment or answer.

MESSAGE

From: Warden O Signe

To: Chief Warden A Signe

We've just finished the Second Section and the Inspector has found that there has been excessive and unjustified damage illegally caused to the Retha Protected Reserve and that the species responsible is the humans. What does illegally mean? For that don't they have to be a responsible sentient species? In which case shouldn't they be here?

There are six of us in the team. Myself, Prima who is Assistant Warden, Hoagfir who is Technical, Majurah Kikbal who is Senior Ecologist and two juniors Onuraga and Kem Mi Su who seem very good.

We were planning to leave earlier but I'm not sure there is much we can start on until we know what we are expected to be doing. It seemed best to stay here so we can hear all the evidence and be around in case the Director needs anything. He still doesn't seem keen to criticise Idreji.

Everyone shares our loathing for these humans. Don't they understand what they have done? Are they advanced sentient or not? **Olte.**

From: Ch.Wdn A Signe.

To: Wdn O Signe.

I suspect the Director is sensitive to the criticism that he should have done more. If the Inspection before ours had been done properly and if he had arranged a couple of drop in checks this might not have happened. **Da.**

Private Journal

Peti came back.

"Sorry to be so long. If you want to go yourself you could get away now before the next Synod. I wasn't sure whether you wanted to go to Retha as well as the Hospital Ship but you should be able to manage both if you want and still get back in time. I've looked through your commitments and there is nothing Setar or one of the other Commissioners can't do. They are going to have to get used to it soon anyway. But are you sure you are up to it?"

I was a bit miffed by that. Of course I'm up to it! Only Peti could talk to me like that. She's been running me for what seems like ever.

It made me realise that I hadn't really thought to check that she would be alright when I retired. I felt very guilty. Somehow I had assumed she would just stay with Setar.

MESSAGE
From: Chief Warden A Signe
To: Warden O Signe.
What you said about the 'illegally' is interesting. I'm not sure whether this has been thought out. If there is a species on a reserve that has got out of control, and there appears no natural solution, then the Directorate are allowed to do a cull up to 20%.
If it's more than that, which I've never heard happen before, you have to apply to the Council which is what we are doing here. But to suggest the damage is illegal suggests that the species involved is responsible or advanced sentient and knows what it's doing. In which case shouldn't they have been given notice and given the opportunity to respond or at the very least offered the opportunity to remedy the damage? **Da**

From: Wdn. O Signe
To: Ch.Wdn. A Signe.
Will anyone raise it? **Olte**

From: Ch.Wdn. A Signe
To: Wdn O Signe.
I don't think most of them will be worrying about it too much. If they are anything like us they will just want to get on and get rid of these creatures. What the Commissioners will make of it is a different matter. My problem is I can't work out how to cull them without destroying the whole planet. We've never done anything on this scale. In fact we never had to do much. I'd like to think that shows we were doing

our job right but probably it was because there was always an almost perfect balance between species. We were really only there to protect the planet from outsiders. We weren't there to harm the indigenous species. We didn't see it as our role to interfere. This problem has only arisen because one species has destroyed that balance. **Da.**

From: Wdn. O Signe
To: Ch.Wdn. A Signe.
Idreji aren't going to get away with this are they?
Olte

From: Ch.Wdn. A Signe
To: Wdn O Signe.
Probably. **Da**

From: Wdn. O Signe
To: Ch.Wdn. A Signe.
Isn't there something you can do? Is the original Inspector still alive? **Olte**

From: Ch.Wdn. A Signe
To: Wdn O Signe.
Yes. **Da**

From: Wdn. O Signe
To: Ch.Wdn. A Signe.
Couldn't you contact her? **Olte**

From: Ch.Wdn. A Signe
To: Wdn O Signe.
No. **Da**

From: Wdn. O Signe
To: Ch.Wdn. A Signe.
Why? **Olte**

From: Ch.Wdn. A Signe
To: Wdn O Signe.
She's the Cygnareina. There is no way a message from me would ever get to her. **Da**

From: Wdn. O Signe
To: Ch.Wdn. A Signe.
Was she the Cygnareina when she carried out the Inspection? **Olte**

From: Ch.Wdn. A Signe
To: Wdn O Signe.
No. She was just a Commissioner then, they call themselves the Sisters. Her mother was the Cygnareina. **Da**

From: Wdn. O Signe
To: Ch.Wdn. A Signe.
Did you know? **Olte**

From: Ch.Wdn. A Signe
To: Wdn O Signe.
No. **Da**

S

Private Journal

Avsa and I carried on as long as we could but we knew it couldn't go on for ever. Finally we really had no choice but to return to the temporary base ship. The Director's calls were becoming more frequent and insistent.

We thought we'd still have some time together, that we would just report back and then go off again. Instead, as soon as we got there, Avsa was sent off to do something urgent which he was supposed to have done long before. I stayed around for a while praying he would return. I had the excuse of taking evidence from the other staff but in all honesty that didn't take long and it was starting to become embarrassing. I was the Inspector and I had finished the Inspection, why was I still there? Finally I had no choice but to leave. I never saw him again. It was only when I was half way home I realized I was pregnant and had to stop to lay the egg.

I wrote the report when I got back. I recommended protected status and the Sisters duly granted it at their next Synod.

Inspector (contd).   My first question is if we don't do anything what will happen?

Dr Ryw Kryg.   In the last fifty years the humans' population has doubled. They have cut down half of the remaining forests.   Something like a fifth of other species have become or are very close to extinction. The total number of other animals, birds and marine creatures has been reduced by at least half.

They have created more damage and produced more pollution in the last fifty years than all species put together, including themselves, since the planet was created.

They are constantly fighting each other. They have nuclear and chemical weapons that can destroy the whole planet many times over.

The more of them there are the more the risk of infections from a variety of diseases which could wipe out most, if not all of them.

If their population continues to increase as it has there just won't be enough food and their cities will run out of water.

If I was a medical Doctor I'd say that, even if we don't do anything, their chances of survival are, to say the very least, not good. I think our only worry must be that, whilst they carry on and destroy themselves, they will destroy everything else as well.

Hanna Langed.   The amount of food they need to produce is now so great they can't allow any other species to eat it. They kill any species that does. For instance the insecticides that have been mentioned previously. It doesn't occur to them that those insects are as much entitled to live as them. They are completely focussed on their own needs. They think that it is their right to kill any animals or birds which are eating 'their' crops or seals or cormorants that are eating 'their' fish.

Few of them realise that they are all part of the natural balance of nature and that if you destroy one species even something apparently as insignificant to them as an insect, it may have effects elsewhere. Humans are probably one of the very few species that wouldn't be missed. They are really just parasites.

If their population goes on increasing as it is then, on their own prediction, their numbers will go up from its present figure of seven billion to at least eleven billion in fifty years. If that happens they will have no choice but to use up all the remaining natural land for cultivation or building. There may be just a few bits left in the very inaccessible parts of the planet but not much more. It is a vicious circle. The more of them there are the more food they will need but the less room there will be to grow it.

Inspector. Why has this creature's population increased so much in just the last fifty years?

Dr Vynack. It is partly due to the reduction in infantile mortality because they now have much better hygiene and medical care in pregnancy. And because of better sanitation – at least in some areas. It is also partly due to people living longer – as the result of their development of vaccines against infectious diseases and

129

of antibacterial drugs such as antibiotics. But mainly it's due to their increased standard of living over the last fifty years.

I came across a piece on their communications system by one of their experts which suggests that the growth in the human population is now slowing down naturally and may even "start to reduce" within a few generations. It is true that there does seem to be evidence in one or two countries of smaller families but this is very very recent. It seems to be partly due to improved contraception, partly due to increased prosperity and education and partly because parents are now more confident that any children they have will survive childhood so they don't need to have so many.

I should say there is also some evidence that the pollution they are now producing – in the air they breathe and the food they eat and the water they drink – is causing infertility particularly in males.

But I don't think that is making much difference. Their population is still increasing.

Inspector. Don't they realise that they are destroying the planet not just for all the other species but also for themselves?

Thawlying Thernjie. Some of them have. As we have heard from the earlier evidence they have even investigated and plotted their own pollution. There are organisations and political parties that campaign to do something about it but mainly they just argue that they should try to produce and consume less. They aren't really doing anything about population.

Inspector. Don't they understand that there are too many of them? If what Dr Kryg has just said is right, if they are causing this amount of pollution now, what will it be like with eleven billion? Even if they aren't bothered about any other species don't they worry about the effect it would have on them?

Thawlying Thernjie. Some may, but not most. It is regarded as their right to have children, not a privilege. Whilst this species is very inventive it is not, as others have said, really advanced in other respects. They still have the urge to procreate mindlessly.

Assistant Dean Ni Jerp. I know we think what they are doing is wrong but we mustn't overlook the fact that they are the most inventive species that we have ever found.   That may be because they are physically comparatively primitive, so they have had to develop these aids and tools in a way that we more advanced species have not, but the fact is they have.

The most remarkable is their development of computing and communications technology. If they can do that in less than twenty years what will they do in another twenty?

Thawlying Thernjie. Yes, but at what cost?

Awosyre Pahmbach. They are a self important little species. They don't do anything naturally. They think they can solve all problems by inventing or developing more tools, chemicals, medicines or whatever. They have produced tools for everything. To them they have become the sign of their own superiority. They had to wear clothes originally because they cannot control their own body temperatures and would freeze in colder climes or burn in hotter ones but it has now become so much part of their thinking that they wear them anyway. It makes them feel superior to animals. They are judged by their possessions. For instance the size of their home or automobile. There are even right and wrong clothes depending upon who you are and where you are and the time of day. Someone who evolved the ability to control their own temperature and walked around naked would be arrested for indecency. Most of them eat food with utensils. They won't use their fingers. It seems to make them feel they have risen above dumb animals.

They have now invented so many tools to compensate for their limited physical abilities they have probably stopped their own physical evolution. Instead of breeding in resistance to illnesses they are inventing drugs and treatments for them, so they are never going to go away and will be passed on from one generation to the next. These drugs and treatments may have extended their life span by a quarter in the last fifty years but all they are doing is keeping themselves alive longer. They are not significantly extending their real active healthy life span. Their bodies are still wearing out by the time they are seventy.

What is of even more concern is they are almost certainly stopping any other creatures on Retha from evolving into advanced sentient status. We don't know how many other species there are that would be capable of doing that. Birds are by far the most advanced physically. Look at the distances they can fly and their advanced navigation skills and their ability to anticipate weather.

Most of us might think that all those birds are basically the same anatomically and physiologically. In fact the evolutionary difference between them is amazing. Some have the ability to hover. Some can take off and land vertically. Some can dive straight into the sea and swim underwater. Some can remain permanently in flight. Many have adapted their beaks or wings or stomachs so they are better able to catch and digest their particular sources of food. Virtually all are, in their own way, physically far more developed than these humans. There are similar differences when it comes to mammals. For example their respiratory systems can be completely different depending on whether they are a species that needs to move very fast for a short distance to catch their prey or whether they need long distance endurance.

Some fish or marine mammals are possible sentient species. The advantage they have is that they have suffered marginally less persecution by humans, particularly those in deep waters. There may well be species capable of advanced thought and communication down there.

The problem is that these humans can't distinguish between superiority and dominance. They will kill anything that they see as a threat. They don't realise that strength and intelligence brings responsibility.

Director Erigh Jonsen. On that point I am afraid we have some very sad news.

We have just heard from Professor Andemus's team. They have now returned to Base. Unfortunately Professor Andemus was caught in a net from one of these creatures deep sea fishing trawlers.

Her team were not able to do anything but one of them was filming at the time and caught the incident on film.

You are welcome to view it if you like but I must warn you it is very distressing.

I have received from Idreji a copy of what, I understand, are news photos from the port this trawler returned to. They extracted them from this species communications system. They show Professor Andemus's body being looked at and photographed by onlookers. They apparently regard her as some prehistoric sea creature which was assumed to be long extinct.

Ulrigh Careighra, Secretary of State for External Affairs, Government of the Outuin.

If I may come in here Sir. As I understand you've already explained we will be going out of communication very shortly and will not return for some time. Certainly not in my lifetime.

As some of you will be aware we are a marine species. We are one of very few sub aqua species to be designated a Responsible Sentient Species. In our view this is not because fish have more difficulty in evolving advanced sentient abilities. It is because we have difficulty communicating with land or air based species so we are rarely identified. To be more blunt it is easy to forget there could be intelligent life under the sea.

As a marine sentient species we accept our responsibility to protect all marine life both on our own planet and, where we can, throughout the known Cosmos. We have seen far too often examples of natural laws being ignored or flouted when it comes to us. This may be more due to ignorance rather than deliberate but that is no help to those species, sentient or otherwise, that are affected. We have already heard of the industrial level fishing that this species undertakes.

What right do they think they have to kill their fellow creatures on this scale? I understand some of the fish caught are just processed to manufacture fertiliser. It is obscene.

These current problems were created by a land based species. We are concerned that if the Directorate were to adopt a non specific remedy to eradicate them it may destroy other species as well, in particular those who live under the sea. They were in no way responsible for what has happened. Any remedy must be specific. It cannot be allowed to damage all the other innocent species, sentient or otherwise.

What we have just heard about Professor Andemus is truly sad. It merely goes to confirm what I have been trying to say. I had the privilege of meeting Professor Andemus some time ago when she visited our planet. As a marine species we were proud of her. She will be sorely missed.

Private Journal

Up to now the proceedings had been very restrained. There had been few interruptions or even questions. Probably because everyone had had the chance to read the papers beforehand.

Now it was becoming more fraught. A loathing towards this species was starting to come through in what each witness said.

Should the Inspector have declared it illegal? Isn't that going to cause problems? I suppose it could be said that the illegality was on the part of Idreji for allowing all this to happen but they aren't going to like that. Could we have given notice to these creatures? Are our standard public notices legally sufficient? Could we have posted them on their communications system? Did we know about that then? By calling it illegal does that mean we are now obliged to contact them? Is that why the Inspector did it?

COUNCIL of COMMISSIONERS

Retha Inquiry Transcript CONTINUED

Inspector. Thank you Secretary of State. We share all you say about Professor Andemus.

My next question is are this species doing anything about the damage they are causing?

Dr Ryw Kryg. I went into this a bit as part of my research. It is obvious, from all we now know, that this species have prospered at the expense of the rest of their planet, particularly over the last fifty or one hundred years. You have already heard enough about the damage they have caused so I don't need to repeat it. They are doing one or two things to try to put it right but not very much. Really they only seem to be playing at it. It's as if they want to be seen to be doing something but at the same time still want to carry on as they are.

They have become fixated with 'carbon dioxide' or 'CO_2' or 'carbon' emissions which they say are creating climate change which is damaging the environment. That is probably true but it is a drop in the ocean compared with all the other damage they are doing. They are spending lots of money, time and energy coming up with ways of reducing these carbon emissions. They call it a 'low carbon economy'.

The 'wind farms', which may have been the cause of Chief Warden Avsa Signe's injuries, are an example. If you take into account the short life span of the turbines and all the energy expended in constructing them and their unreliable output, which depends on what wind there is, it is very doubtful if they will really make any difference. Most of these turbines will have a life of less than thirty years so they will then have to build yet more. The old ones will probably just be abandoned and left to clutter up the planet for ever, like everything else these creatures do.

I have difficulty understanding why they think climate change alone is the greatest threat to the planet. Obviously it isn't something you want to happen if you can help it but, even on their worse predictions, it's not likely to be very significant – particularly in comparison to all the other climate changes Retha has seen in the past – ice ages for instance. In fact, like most climate change, whilst some parts of the planet will be adversely affected others will actually benefit.

Don't misunderstand me, of course CO_2 emissions are something they should be worried about, in common with all the other things they spew out into the air – carbon monoxide, sulphur dioxide, nitrogen oxides, ammonia, particulates etc, etc, etc. What I take issue with is that they are characterising carbon emissions and climate change as the major, if not the only, problem. It's all the other stuff they are doing which is just as serious.

This obsession with carbon emissions is curious. Trees and plants on Retha need CO_2. They 'breathe' – or more accurately absorb or sequester it – in much the same way as humans, and all the other mammals on Retha, breathe oxygen. Cutting down trees releases enormous amounts of CO_2. If they were really worried about carbon emissions and climate change they would stop clearing any more forests. They should actually be replacing all the forest they have cleared. Instead they are still cutting down even more – to burn for fuel and as building materials! They think that is 'greener' and 'sustainable'!

In fairness they have taken a few small steps to reduce their pollution and waste but the real total is still increasing, not decreasing. They talk a lot about the need to reduce energy consumption but the total amount they need still increases every year as their standard of living increases. More and more cars, trucks and planes, more electrical equipment, more heating and air cooling, more and more complicated communication systems etc, etc, etc. They didn't need a fraction of that fifty years ago.

They think they are helping by producing electricity from "green" projects like hydro-electric dams, solar farms, tidal barrages and wind turbines but they ignore the damage these projects do to the environment and to other species. A barrage across a tidal inlet means that the salt water fish and invertebrates die off. So the ducks, waders and seabirds will have nothing to feed on and a whole ecosystem dies. Imagine the amount of energy required to manufacture the millions of tons of concrete needed to build a barrage or dam.

As I say, the weird thing is that they describe all this as "green". They really do seem to believe that constructing hundreds of wind turbines or solar farms or tidal turbines, covering vast areas, with all the accompanying cabling and pylons not to mention the resulting damage to the land or sea bed and to bird and other species is "saving the planet".

All these things have a limited life span. They will then just be left to rot and they'll have to build new ones somewhere else to replace them. All they are really doing is spreading their urban pollution wider and wider into otherwise unspoilt areas. The fact is that, to them, 'saving the planet' simply means keeping it going for humans. They aren't worried about anything else.

Private Journal

Out of curiosity I flicked on to Dr Kryg's photo. I often find that creatures who, at a distance come across as intimidating and forceful, turn out to be mild furry little creatures when you get to meet them.

Not this time. Dr Kryg looked just as she comes across. A more formidable and forthright reptilian you couldn't imagine. Someone you know, just to look at her, is destined to end up as Dean of a major university.

COUNCIL of COMMISSIONERS
Retha Inquiry Transcript CONTINUED

Inspector (contd).   Is there anything more they could do?

Dr Ryw Kryg.   Of course there is. They should be stopping any further deforestation and the clearing of any remaining uncultivated land. They should allow cleared areas to return to a natural state and re-establish themselves. That would really help sort the CO_2 problem and would help endangered species. They should stop using plastic. They should stop fishing the seas in the way they do. They should stop building on yet more land. They should stop using pesticides. The trouble is they can't do any of those things whilst their population continues to increase.

They have to cut down more and more forests and fish more fish just to feed and house the extra mouths. They have to use pesticides to produce the food in the quantity they need it. They can't stop now even if they realise the damage it is doing. If they are allowed to continue breeding as they are they will need more and more land to support the increasing population.

They use CO_2 as a convenient scapegoat. If they are seen to be worrying about that it takes attention away from everything else – the destruction of the forests, all the waste they create, the destruction of plant and animal life. To put it simply, the problem is not global warming or CO_2. It is that their population is out of control. Everything else is just a symptom.

Hannah Langed. They are continuing to cut down enormous areas – millions of acres of virgin rain forest – for palm oil plantations. They use palm oil in the manufacture of foods, soaps and lots of other products because its cheap and easy to grow. They aren't bothered that these plantations destroy the natural habitats of countless different species including some of the rarest on the planet such as orang-utan and tigers. They aren't even bothered that they have robbed the local people of their land.

As I mentioned in my evidence they are using this palm oil to produce ethanol! In other words they are actually cutting down the rain forest to produce ethanol to use as a 'green' fuel. They claim it's better for the planet. I suspect it's better for those humans who are making lots of money out of it.

Inspector. Are any of them worrying about their population? Incidentally if anyone is having difficulty on the various measurements that are being quoted there is a convertor on the Council's screen.

Thawlying Thernjie. There really isn't much evidence of any real desire to restrict their own population. They are happy to cull other creatures. They drastically control species which eat their trees, grass or crops but they aren't doing anything about themselves.

Inspector. Can they?

Olwen Slliga. Oh yes. They have developed very good methods of birth control in the last fifty years. There is no reason why they shouldn't restrict their families to one per couple which is what a lot of us have to do. If everyone can only have one child the population will drop quite quickly. My people are now allowed to have two per couple but this still means our population will continue to reduce slightly. Even this has only come in in my lifetime. I'm an only child.

Thawlying Thernjie. We have only found one country on Retha that tried to introduce the one child rule but no-one else gave them any support. There even seems to be the feeling that doing that is actually wrong and 'inhuman'. These creatures seem to think that it is everyone's 'human right' to have as many children as they want. This seems to be a deeply held belief.

In most of their cultures they believe that taking human life is the ultimate sin. In many cultures abortion is a crime. In some even contraception is discouraged. There is one religion in particular that still tries not only to prohibit abortion but also to discourage contraception.

Inspector. Why?

Thawlying Thernjie. Historically it was because it wanted to be the largest religion so it encouraged its adherents to have as many children, grandchildren and great grandchildren as possible. Even if that meant they would be born into poverty and that mothers would have to have ten or even fifteen children. They still tell them that having an abortion is a sin and if they do they won't go to Heaven, which is where they believe good people go when they die.

Although different religions and societies have differing views on contraception and abortion they all seem to share the same view on euthanasia. Most countries do not allow 'assisted' suicide which is what we would call euthanasia. In other words being able to have assistance to die in a civilised fashion. That is prohibited without question nearly everywhere. It is something they hardly talk about. This may seem totally irrational to us but it seems to be a deeply rooted conviction.

Inspector. Do you mean that they can't even choose when they want to die?

Thawlying Thernjie. In practical terms, yes. If someone helps them by, say, providing drugs or injections they will be prosecuted. It goes back to their fundamental belief in the 'sanctity' of human life. What is sick is that all this only applies to themselves. They are happy to control and kill any other species. There are virtually no laws to prevent that.

It is all very primitive. It is all based upon the belief that they are the superior species.

Inspector. Does that apply even if they are in pain or dying or unable to look after themselves?

Thawlying Thernjie. Yes.

Private Journal

This is barbaric. Are they really saying that they can't choose when they want to retire (as I prefer to call it)? They really are primitive.

I may not have planned long ahead but I always knew I would choose when I went.

What's the point in going on when your body has had enough?

Do they really force their elderly to go through all the pain and misery and probably loneliness of old age? Apart from anything else think of the cost. What's the point of having to struggle financially at the end of your life?

I don't think any Members, in other words recognised Responsible Sentient Species, now prevent anyone from going when they want. If they wish to carry on, until they die naturally, that's up to them but most I know have decided to go in a civilised manner at a time of their own choosing. Some have made the point of having their family and friends around them. Some I have known have even had leaving parties.

COUNCIL of COMMISSIONERS
Retha Inquiry Transcript CONTINUED

Hoagfir Andronkle. I am a Technician with the Conservation Directorate. I have just been appointed Technical Manager of the Retha Warden Service. I have been listening to all the evidence. I hope it's alright if I come in here.

After what the Director said about the links from the Hundil Communications Centre I went onto these human's communications system to see what was on there.

They don't care about any one else. They test new drugs on dogs and rats and mice and chimpanzees before they try them out on themselves because only they matter and 'animals' don't.

They are just bullies. Because they can dominate and kill other species they do. They do it not just to feed themselves but for fun. They shoot migratory birds as they pass over, not to eat but for sport in the same way as they chase and hunt animals, like deer, wolves, bears, jackals and foxes.

If they think that another species numbers have become too large they cull them. They wouldn't understand if anyone did it to them.

They farm billions of animals in disgusting conditions. They treat them just like crops. They interfere with their breeding so they grow quicker and produce more body weight for less feed.

They grow around fifty billion chickens each year to eat. They house them in horrible little cages. Thirty years ago it took them ninety days to grow one.

Because of selective breeding, they've now got that down to forty days. That means these chickens are no longer able to develop a normal skeleton so they are in constant pain.

They transport animals enormous distances in horrible conditions to be killed. Some of the killing methods they use are revolting.

In the last fifty years they have reduced the number of fish in the sea by something between fifty and seventy percent, depending on whose figures you use. They kill elephants and rhinoceros just for their tusks and horns and they have killed whales, almost to extinction, just for their oil.

Private Journal

I flicked up Hoagfir's image on the screen. As I expected this terrifyingly large four legged dog appeared. They say the Borredans' bark is worse than their bite but I wouldn't like to be the one to try it. He certainly wasn't someone likely to take kindly to being regarded as a dumb animal.

Hanna Langed. We are talking about humans as if they are all rich and technically advanced. But the ordinary ones in the poorer countries still have to worry every day how they are going to get enough food to feed their children. If they cut down a few trees to build a house or to heat it or to cook their food, or to provide space to grow crops can you blame them? You can't blame them if they kill a rare animal for that day's meal or if they take money from richer humans on the other side of the planet to kill an elephant. None of this would be a problem if there were less of them.

Inspector. Aren't their Governments doing anything about population growth?

Thawlying Thernjie. Not really. Most of their countries are now democracies which means, everyone over a certain age has an equal say in who governs them. The result is that these Governments will do what the majority want and will never do anything unpopular. Restriction of population is not a vote winner.

It's worse than that, many Governments still encourage women to have children. In many countries, if they are pregnant, their medical fees are paid. In some they get paid maternity leave. Some Governments even pay allowances to the parents for each child they have while they are growing up. The more children they have the more they get. In some places they even pay for the father to have time off work when the baby is born. Obviously this mainly applies to richer countries.

Inspector. Why ever should they want to do that?

Thawlying Thernjie. They think it brings in votes.

Hoagfir Andronkle. If someone can't afford to look after their own children why are they having them?

Thawlying Thernjie. Quite.

Inspector. Are you saying that everyone has an equal say?

Thawlying Thernjie. Yes. They call them voters. Everyone has an equal vote.

Inspector. Irrespective of what they contribute?

Thawlying Thernjie. Yes.

Inspector. Doesn't that lead to anarchy?

Thawlying Thernjie. Yes. That is effectively the problem.

Inspector. If, as everyone says, they are intelligent and resourceful why haven't they worked out they can't go on like this?

Thawlying Thernjie. Obviously some have but no-one really wants to hear. It isn't a popular message. Only humans have votes and they aren't going to vote for anything that doesn't suit them. Most of them aren't really bothered about what is happening to the planet. They really don't think it affects them.

Their Governments aren't doing anything because they'll lose votes. Arguably their societies are now so big and complex they are virtually ungovernable. In democracies Governments are only in power for a few years. Why do anything unpopular?

Hoagfir Andronkle.   Oh come on let's get real. All of us have had to face this. Why should they be different? My species are only allowed to have one child and even then only if we can show we can afford to support it. We weren't given any choice by the Council of Commissioners even though what we were doing to our planet wasn't anything like as bad as this. Our rules are very strict. Each of us can only have one child whether that is in a permanent relationship or not. Once we've had a child neither the mother nor the father can have any more. If you split up you won't be allowed to have children with anyone else. One thing we've noticed is that everyone takes a lot more care choosing their mate.

Dr Vynack.   In fairness a lot of their countries are very poor and their Governments haven't got the resources to provide contraception let alone enforce population control.

Assistant Dean Ni Jerp.   I think it must be said that there are quite a lot of humans, some influential, who do believe that something must be done about over-population but they don't seem to be able to talk about it openly. Perhaps we should do something to try to help them.

Private Journal

I felt tears pouring down my face.

They asked to see me. Two uncomfortable, worried looking Doctors.

"Madam" said the first one. "The egg is a male. What do you want us to do with it? Do you want us to destroy it?"

The other said *"How did this happen. Was it unplanned?"*

The first gave her a filthy look as if to say *"You can't ask her things like that"*. But to be fair they were entitled to ask so no-one could blame them.

I got them to package the egg up again as it was when I brought it back home. I dropped in the leg ring my mother gave me when I was born.

I addressed it to Avsa and put a note in with it 'We had a son. I am not allowed to keep him. I hope you can. Love Mitzo' and passed it through to the Universal Mail. I never heard any more. I never knew whether Avsa received it and if he did whether he was allowed to keep it.

MESSAGE
From: Warden O Signe
To: Chief Warden A Signe
Was she my mother? **Olte**

From: Chief Warden A Signe
To: Warden O Signe
Yes **Da**

From: Warden O Signe
To: Chief Warden A Signe
How did you get me? **Olte**

From: Chief Warden A Signe
To: Warden O Signe
You came in a box with a note from her. I've still got it. It said she wasn't allowed to keep you. I sat on you myself. You took a long time to hatch. **Da**

Inspector. Why can't the rich countries do something?

Dr Vynack. No one country is going to take the initiative. None of them trust each other. One country doesn't want another to get more powerful than them so no-one is going to take the first step to reduce their population. Another reason is that their economies are now so complex they are dependent on 'growth'. In other words more and more of them consuming more things and paying more taxes.

The resentment that the less developed countries have against the richer ones also mustn't be overlooked. It's the richer ones that have taken the most and caused most of the damage to the planet through their excessive consumption. The poorer ones don't see why they shouldn't have what the richer ones have.

All this plundering of the planet has given the richer nations a higher standard of living. In those countries you now have a whole generation who have never known hunger and have never had to worry where their food is coming from. Their children will not be so lucky.

Those in the very poor countries still suffer famine and starvation. For many of them everything is still just a matter of survival.

Inspector. I'm interested in what you said about the economies they have created. They seem to be far more complex than anything we see elsewhere in the

Cosmos.   Does that make population reduction more difficult?

Dr Vynack.   Obviously there will be short term economic problems if they systematically reduce their population.   As I've said their economies are based on growth – producing more and earning more and paying more taxes.   But that is really only because they have become totally preoccupied with trying to satisfy the increasing demands of an expanding population.

If their population is reduced there may be short term adverse economic affects, for example on land prices, but they already have quite dramatic upturns and downturns in their economies anyway.   After they've got over that the economic advantages of not having to constantly build more houses, schools, hospitals, roads, sewers, ports, airports, dams, power stations, flood defences and all the other things they have to do at the moment will make them all better off and certainly a lot happier.

Inspector.   Surely it must be possible to show them that they can't go on like this, and that if they do their children and grandchildren face a very grim future.

Assistant Dean Ni Jerp.   If I may come in here.   I understand everyone's natural concerns as to what this species has done but I do feel we should at least be trying to contact them to give them the chance to put things right.

In our research we were amazed by what they can do. They have invented far more than anything you see anywhere else in the Universe.   Whether they need to is a different matter.

If they make one thing someone else then betters it and then someone else does it in a different way. They have millions of different products for their work, their home, their clothing. As far as we can see it is really only being done to create employment and to keep people occupied. It certainly consumes vast amounts of the planet's resources and produces an enormous amount of waste. But having said that, it would be a pity if we couldn't find a way to harness their technical skills for the benefit of the whole of the Cosmos. If they have the skills to do what they are doing now they have the skills to do it without destroying their planet.

They have inquiring minds. They want to look into everything. The creation of the Universe, their own make up, the make up of their planet. What they don't seem to be able to do is to face up to the damage they are causing.

I strongly urge that we make some attempt to contact them.

Inspector.   Do they realise that there are other sentient species in the Universe?

Assistant Dean Ni Jerp.   That's a bit strange. They write about us in books and films.   They call us 'extraterrestrials' or 'creatures from outerspace' or 'aliens'.   They have tens of thousands of adventure books and thousands of 'science fiction' or 'sci-fi' films about us but when anyone seriously suggests we really do exist they are laughed at. Interestingly these books and films all assume any visitors from other worlds will be hostile and warlike. I think that's probably more a reflection on themselves.

Thawlying Thernjie. That's certainly true. Others have mentioned these creatures' treatment of other indigenous species but their treatment of each other is just as brutal. They are constantly at war. There is never a moment when what we would regard as a major war isn't going on somewhere on the planet. The destruction these cause is unbelievable. They don't seem to be able to live at peace even with their fellow creatures. Whether this is as a result of too many of them living too close together, or just part of their normal character I don't know.

Private Journal

I looked at the faces of all the regulators, bureaucrats, lawyers and academics that had given evidence. Even though there were lots of different species from all over the Cosmos a less warlike group you couldn't find. In fact I can't remember when I last came across anyone like that (apart from Hoagfir!). Thankfully we seem to have out grown it.

Inspector.   Does anyone else have any final comments?

Dr Ryw Kryg.   I know I've probably already said enough but I'd like to come back briefly. If it is decided to try to communicate with these creatures what they need to grasp is that they can't go on as they are. The things they are currently doing, to mitigate the damage they are causing, are only gestures. They aren't going to make any difference. The only thing that will make a difference is if they cut their population drastically. If they do, they will be much better off whether they are from rich or poor countries. If their population is less, the land they need is less and their impact on the planet is less. Provided they are responsible they should be able to continue to do all the other things they want.

Dr Vynack.   Our ultimate duty is to ensure the basic balance between all species. We aren't there to judge. You will always have one species which kills another species for their food.   That is unfortunately part of natural existence but the balance should be self regulating. If one species wipes out its main food source then it will inevitably wipe itself out. To some extent that is what is happening here but on a scale we could not imagine. This is not one species threatening say one or two others. These creatures are threatening everything.

We have to make them understand that this planet isn't theirs. They must reduce their population to the level that they can then live in harmony with their fellow creatures. This doesn't have to be something they should be afraid of. Many of us have been through something similar. Not having children isn't as awful as it may seem. It is certainly a lot cheaper. Particularly if none of your taxes are going to pay for those who do.

Hoagfir Andronkle. For goodness sake, the problem is just that there are too many of them. It is as simple as that. Unless we do something they are just going to go on as they are. It's no good thinking we can rationalise with them.

President Henk O Kang. I think there is one other important point that needs to be made. There is disturbing evidence that this species may see expansion into the rest of the Universe or at least their galaxy as the solution to their overpopulation. They must certainly be disabused of any idea that they may have that they can solve their problems by colonising somewhere else.

If they can't be trusted to look after their own planet we certainly mustn't allow them to ruin another one.

Inspector. Thank you. Now if I may, I want to talk about remedies. If the Council were mindful to grant a S427 Order has the Directorate considered how it might be implemented?

Director Erigh Jonsen. We haven't had long to think about this so we are still at a very early stage and I can only give you our initial thoughts. We are certainly not yet in a position to commit ourselves to one particular solution.

There has never been the need for a cull on this scale before and no-one has any experience of it. As you may know the Directorate is allowed to carry out a cull of up to twenty percent of the population of any species on a reserve without requiring the Council's consent. We have rarely, if ever, needed to do even that. We have certainly never previously applied for a S427 order. The reason we are doing so now is that we will need help to implement it. If the Council should grant a Section 427 Order we would ask that they give us some freedom in selecting the most appropriate remedy.

These creatures now have no natural predators. They have eradicated those that there were. If any others were to be introduced they would eradicate them also. So they are really only vulnerable to two things. Firstly, catastrophes natural or otherwise, such as crop failure, chemical and nuclear wars, nuclear accidents, storms, floods, earthquakes and volcanoes. Even then those will normally have only limited effects. Secondly, disease. This is their main vulnerability but they are increasingly finding ways of preventing or curing them. One hundred of their years ago most people, even in the richest areas, would expect to die by around the age of seventy predominantly from illnesses such as pneumonia. Now, mainly because of the discovery of anti bacterial drugs they can easily live to ninety. That is, of course, one of the factors behind the increase in their numbers.

We have considered all the possible solutions we have been able to think of and you will see these are outlined in our report. Some of them are a little outlandish. Although I will summarise them all briefly for the sake of completeness, I have got to say that in practical terms there is probably only one real option open to us. All the other suggestions are a bit theoretical and impracticable.

The first we looked at is some form of disease or blight that kills the food they grow. There have been examples of this in their history – the potato famine caused by Phytophthora is an example. We haven't closed our minds to this one but the general view is that it will be difficult to do on a large enough scale. To be effective we would need to do it for most if not all of the main staple crops – say wheat, rice and corn and possibly potatoes, cassava and soya bean - all preferably at the same time. We aren't sure how we could achieve this. The problem is not only in producing several different plant diseases but also finding the means of spreading them. This may be beyond us.

The second was a black cloud. It is not necessarily as impossible as it sounds but it is not really a realistic solution. I included it only because it was raised. There is the capability within the science community to produce one of the size needed comparatively easily. This planet is not a large one. As you may know once you've created a black cloud, if you simply park it between a planet and its sun, everything that needs light to survive will die. Obviously they don't come cheap and we would need the Council to fund and organise it. It would also probably take at least one hundred of Retha's years to get one in place. However the real point is that it will kill virtually everything, not just these humans.

The third is an asteroid. A meteorite would be too small. Again we only included this because it is a theoretical possibility but it really isn't really feasible. It is very hit and miss if you'll forgive the pun. From a practical point of view I understand it isn't too difficult to divert a meteorite but an asteroid is a bit more complicated. Even then until it hits you won't know the exact result. It might kill all life. It might only have a limited effect. Any damage it causes would affect all species not just humans. It depends to an extent on the size. There is evidence that Retha has been hit by at least one large asteroid in its past history which seems to have wiped out virtually everything.

In the case of both black clouds and asteroids, sea living creatures probably have the greatest chance of survival.

This leaves us with some form of disease which is our fourth option. It is probably the only one that has any real possibility of destroying most if not all of this species without annihilating everything else. It is probably best if Doktor Cehndik, who is Head of our Central Laboratories, explains this.

Doktor Cehndik. Thank you. What we have looked at is the possibility of introducing a viral or bacterial infection specific to humans. Can I emphasise we are still at a very early stage on this.

To be successful it needs to be a pathogen which will kill humans but not other species. It has to be one to which they have no natural immunity and no effective vaccine or medicine and it has to be capable of being introduced on a mass scale – in other words it has to be highly infectious. Initially we thought the chances of achieving all of this was small.

We are now a little more optimistic. We are getting good at accessing this species internet – what they call their communication system. There are vast numbers of medical research papers of one kind or another on it. These include ones on the large numbers of pathogens that these creatures have identified – mainly as part of the process of producing vaccines and drugs to counteract or destroy them.

The problem is that they now have a defence to most of them. Our initial idea was to re-engineer one or more of those viruses or bacteria into something sufficiently new they would have no defences to it. The difficulty is that the re-engineering itself could make the pathogen less effective or not effective at all or possibly make it dangerous to other species as well. We wouldn't know until we actually started using it which might be a bit too late. Whilst we haven't dismissed that option we are also looking to see if there are still any existing pathogens which are highly infectious to them, but not to other species, and to which they still have little or no immunity or defence.

We are considering a number of possibilities. Our initial view is that whilst it will need specialised resources and significant funding it should be possible to synthesise at least one of these.

Because they now all live so close together and lots of them travel all round the planet, the right pathogen could, if it is really infectious, spread naturally worldwide in a very short time. Whether it will kill twenty percent or ninety percent of the human population is not something we can control.

I've got to say that there are risks and we won't know whether it does work and doesn't affect other species until we try it. We could possibly do a small trial to begin with but there is the risk that will just give them time to develop medicines or vaccinations to protect themselves from it.

Assistant Dean Ni Jerp.   I find this totally uncivilised. Are we really suggesting that we should eradicate this whole species?

Hoagfir Andronkle.   Why not, its what they've been doing. They have wiped out other species without any thought.   They systematically cull other animals like deer, badgers, koala, wolves, seals and cormorant as well as birds of prey. They deliberately gave a horrible infection to rabbits just to get the numbers down. The only species they don't control is themselves.

Assistant Dean Ni Jerp.   If I may continue? Doesn't this go against all we stand for. Aren't we there to help those species that want to evolve to do so, whilst protecting those who don't?

President Henk O Kang.   What protection did you provide to the billions of creatures who have died because of the loss of their habitats or who have been killed by this species for food or fun? If you'd done your job properly this would never have happened.

Advokate Otto Slaborg.   Sir, I really must protest. Surely this matter warrants intelligent debate.

Inspector.   I agree. Please continue Assistant Dean Ni Jerp.

Assistant Dean Ni Jerp.   Thank you. Whatever the cause of this problem we do not accept that criticism. However we have got to start from where we are now and look for a solution that is right for all species, zoological or botanical including these humans.

Hoagfir Andronkle.   Why?   They are thugs and criminals.

Inspector.   Enough. Assistant Dean Ni Jerp please continue.

Assistant Dean Ni Jerp.   I am still of the view that rather than a cull we should try to communicate with them and put it to them that they must remedy the situation without further delay.

Hoagfir Andronkle.   That's ridiculous, they won't do anything.   Anyway what does "remedy the situation" mean?

Assistant Dean Ni Jerp.   It means that they will have to reduce their population significantly and do it very quickly. I do think there are indications that they are now aware of the damage they are doing and taking steps to address it.

Dr Ryw Kryg.   That's nonsense. There may be a few of them who are talking about it but no-one is really doing anything. They are still cutting down the forests. They say they are replacing them but for every new tree they plant they are cutting down three. They are bringing more land into cultivation, their population is still increasing, they are building more cities with all that involves. What we want to see is all this stopping and them taking clear steps to drastically reduce their population and allow the planet to start recovering.

Inspector. I think I may have asked this before, but if we do nothing what happens?

Hanna Langed. The most obvious result of over population is starvation. Not simply because increasingly there will not be enough food for everyone, but also because there will not be sufficient surpluses in the good years to set aside for the bad ones. Those could be the result of weather – too hot, too cold, not enough rain or too much rain. There is also the increasing risk of crop disease which is the almost inevitable result of intensive, particularly single crop, cultivation. The same applies to erosion and loss of topsoil. Because there is no safety net, one bad year would kill very large numbers.

Dr Vynack. I personally think the job may be done for us. Their current growth is unsustainable. I think something will happen within a hundred years, possibly less, through disease, war, nuclear or chemical accidents, or simple starvation, which will reduce their population size. For instance if they go on as they are their cities will just run out of water if there is any drought. Over population also increases the risk of disease. Even if we don't introduce an epidemic of some kind the chances are that one, probably several, will occur naturally which will have exactly the same effect.

Alternatively they may well kill themselves or at least a lot of them. They now have enough nuclear and chemical weapons between them to kill the entire population of the planet many times over. Or it could be as a result of some accident or natural phenomenon, like a solar storm, which affects their communication or control systems. Their societies are now so complex it wouldn't take much – say a computer or communication glitch - and the whole thing would come to a stop.

If their electricity goes off they will start dying very quickly. Water and food supplies stop, sewage systems don't work. Lights go off, offices, shops and factories stop. Communications and computer systems pack up. Refrigerators and freezers in shops and homes stop and the food rots. Hospitals can't operate. Fuel pumps stop. Elevators and public transport and airports stop. They would start dying very very quickly.

The problem we keep coming back to is that before that happens they will probably have destroyed everything we value on Retha.

Director Erigh Jonsen. I should have said that we did consider whether we could interfere with their electrical or communication systems or both. You will see this is mentioned in our report but it was only raised at the last moment so we haven't had the opportunity to research it in any detail. Its advantage is that the damage should be limited to the humans but we aren't confident we could do something on a sufficiently large scale to make a significant difference.

Professor Quvvon.   If I may interrupt here on a similar point.   As part of my research, we looked into Retha's climate patterns.   It appears likely that they are due for an ice age.   The last one took up around a third of the planet for tens of thousands of years.   The humans would have no choice but to move into the central belt of the planet which is warmer but there certainly won't be room for all of them.   So that would significantly reduce their population.   At the same time the other parts of the planet would be cleansed of all their pollution and destruction though it would then take thousands of years to recover.

Inspector.   When you say "due for an ice age" what do you mean?

Professor Quvvon.   Oh no, it won't be that soon, it isn't even likely to start for twenty thousand years at least.

Director Erigh Jonsen.   If I may make a final point. Whilst this species thinks they can continue to carry on as they are, they are not going to do anything significant. They may be making half hearted attempts to cut pollution or reduce the destruction of the forests but it will do no more than scratch the surface.   The only thing that will make a difference is a drastic reduction in population.   If they do that their future generations will thank them.   But it's no good them thinking that all they have to do is limit themselves to two children.   For those who do have children the maximum for a very long time will be just one and even then lots of couples will have to be persuaded, probably by financial incentives, to have none. What's stupid, as has been said, is that if they go on as they are these creatures will destroy themselves anyway through starvation, disease or wars. If they reduce their population to sensible levels, so that they can live in harmony with the rest of the planet, they will be a lot better off. They will still be able to carry on making things and doing what they want provided they allow the rest of the planet to return to how it should be. It's not what they are doing, though we would much prefer they weren't, it's the scale of it that has got out of hand. I agree that we should find some way of telling them this.

Inspector. So I am sure I am clear, is it right that what you are saying is that we should give these Humans notice of what we want of them?

Director Erigh Jonsen. Yes.

Advokate Otto Slaborg. I agree.

Inspector. If they don't do anything what then?

Director Erigh Jonsen. Then we should implement a Section 427 cull.

Inspector. Is everyone else agreed?

Advokate Otto Slaborg. Those are now my instructions.

President Henk O Kang. I concur.

MESSAGE

From: Warden O Signe
To: Chief Warden A Signe

The Inquiry is just about to finish. Hoagfir created quite a performance. He really argued with the Assistant Dean from Idreji. I was worried what the Director would think but he seemed happy. I wondered whether they'd fixed it up between them. Didn't Hoagfir work in his private office?

In the end the Director came round to agreeing that we should try to communicate with these creatures. I suppose he realised that there wasn't much choice. Idreji weren't going to agree otherwise. We are just about to move onto the arguments as to how this happened. It will be interesting to see if he says anything then. **Olte.**

From: Chief Warden A Signe
To: Warden O Signe

It looks to me that the Director might have got Idreji to agree to co-operate in return for not making a big thing about their role in all this. He's probably right. It's more important to get something done now rather than row about things which we can't do anything about. **Da**

Inspector. I will now, as promised, take submissions as to how these unfortunate events happened and what could have been done to prevent it. Whilst I am grateful for the attendance of those from the Retha Project at the University of Idreji I note that Idreji has not made anyone available from their Ranger Teams. Would you like to comment on that Advokate Slaborg?

Advokate Otto Slaborg. In view of allegations and possible threats of prosecutions it was thought inappropriate to call them.

Inspector. Can you at least tell us when Idreji last had a permanent Ranger Team on Retha.

Advokate Otto Slaborg. I am instructed that that was about five hundred of Retha's years ago.

Inspector. Are the Ranger Team's routine reports from then available? Do they indicate that the Team were aware of the development of this species – it surely must have been obvious by then.

Advokate Otto Slaborg. I understand those reports have been mislaid or destroyed.

Inspector. What about the staff on that team. Are any of them available to give evidence?

Advokate Otto Slaborg. I understand that none of them are still employed by the University. They were all laid off as part of a Departmental re-organisation on their return from Retha.

Inspector. What about previous reports, say one thousand years ago?

Advokate Otto Slaborg. Alas they seem to have been mislaid or destroyed at the same time.

President Henk O Kang. This is monstrous. Idreji had the Administration of Retha. They asked to have it. It is clear that for at least the last five hundred years they have had no-one down there. The contract stipulated they should have people on base permanently. If they had, this wouldn't have happened. Are they really suggesting that the Retha Project was some form of alternative? Even if it was it seems too little too late.

Advokate Otto Slaborg. I protest Sir. We have heard a number of allegations against my Clients ranging from suggestions that they actually introduced this species to suggestions that they educated or groomed them to suggestions that all this was just some research project. There is absolutely no evidence to justify any of these allegations and I must ask you to make that clear in your Report. The only possible ground for complaint is that if my Client's had had staff on base during the time in question this might have been noticed sooner. We have no way of knowing whether that would have made any difference. As we have heard, the time scales have been so quick it seems likely that no-one could have prevented it.

As to the suggestion that Idreji should have informed the Directorate of the research the Retha Project were doing on these creatures' communication system, may I remind you how recently all this has been. Even the initial results you've heard have only just been written up. There simply was no opportunity to communicate this to the Directorate or anyone else earlier.

President Henk O Kang. This is all wrong. What was the point of Idreji having the Administration of this Reserve if they didn't even bother to have a team on it? I don't want to blow the UWPF's trumpet but we certainly have not experienced any problems like this on the reserves we administer.

Inspector. I think you have both made your views abundantly clear. Unless anyone else has anything to add I will now close this Inquiry. I thank you all for your assistance and contributions. It is my task now to assess all submissions and put forward my recommendations on the appropriate remedies and action to the Commissioners. In view of the urgency I will endeavour to submit my Report to them as quickly as I possibly can.

Thank you.

Inquiry concluded.

MESSAGE
From: Warden O Signe
To: Chief Warden A Signe
We are now at the Base and are getting on with things as best we can but it is difficult to plan until we know what we are supposed to be doing. We haven't heard anything about the Inspector's findings. Have you? The talk is Idreji are delaying things. **Olte**

From: Chief Warden A Signe
To: Warden O Signe
No. **Da**

From: Warden O Signe
To: Chief Warden A Signe
Isn't there anything you can do? Can't you contact her? **Olte**

From: Chief Warden A Signe
To: Warden O Signe
Alright. **Da.**

MESSAGE
From: Avsa Signe
To: HSH
Mitzo *I don't know if you remember me. I was your Guide when you inspected Retha. Things are very bad there now. The Directorate asked for an Inquiry by a Council Inspector. That has finished but we haven't heard anything.*
Is there anything you can do? **Avsa**

§

Private Journal

I messaged Peti to see if she could find out whether the Inspector's Report was now available. She replied later in the day "It's still with the Lawyers whilst they sort out the objections they've received. It hasn't gone to a Commissioner yet".

I told her to notify the Inspectorate that I was calling this one in personally and that I required a copy of the current draft of the Report.

"OK, but someone's nose is going to be put out of joint" she replied.

"Well let's hope it's the Idrejians, they have more noses to put out of joint than the rest of us".

I then had a thought. Was it really Idreji who was holding things up or was all this in fact something to do with funding? It nearly always is.

I messaged Peti and asked her if she could find out who funds culls on Protected Reserves.

She came back "I've checked with the Attorney General's Office. It's a bit complicated but I think the short answer is that the Director can authorise a cull of up to twenty percent but the Directorate would have to fund it themselves. More than that and the Directorate has to apply for a S427 order but if that is approved they are entitled to funding from the Treasury. That is why it isn't often granted. The person I spoke to didn't have to look it up so I think someone else has already asked".

Of course! That's why the Director has gone for a Section 427 order. Even a twenty percent cull would be nearly one and a half billion creatures and he couldn't possibly fund that, let alone seven billion. So he needs the Treasury. That's why its being held up. It isn't just Idreji's objections. It's the Treasury's as well.

I left as soon as the Inspector's Report arrived. The journey was a lot better than I had expected, last time it seemed to go on for ever. I read the Report on the way.

His factual findings were what we would have expected - that there had been excessive and unjustified damage illegally caused to the Retha Reserve and that those responsible were an indigenous species called Homo Sapiens.

He confirmed that they currently had a population of around seven billion and that was still increasing and was estimated to reach eleven billion within fifty years. He confirmed that the damage was still occurring and there was little evidence of any serious attempts being made by this species to prevent or reduce it. He found that the primary cause was that the population of this species had been permitted to get out of control and that a minor reduction would not now make any difference.

He recorded the view of some witnesses that nothing other than an immediate cull would be effective but that the general view was that whilst a Section 427 Order should be granted the Order should be stayed whilst an attempt is made to communicate with this species to give them an opportunity to correct things themselves without the need for any intervention from us.

He detailed the remedies currently available if there was to be a cull. He discussed the question of whether any of them were cost effective and whether there was an argument for doing nothing and letting these creatures destroy, or at least substantially reduce, themselves.

He considered the question of whether the necessary Public Notices of the Inquiry had been given and whether this species was entitled to have been notified of it. He was of the view that in law the position was clear. The Public Notices had been in accordance with the rules and notification only applied to recognised Responsible Sentient Beings which this species was not. He also noted that it was unlikely that they would be entitled to apply for recognition because it was only open to species who could show that they accepted their responsibility to their planet and their fellow species.

He remarked that if recognised Responsible Sentient Beings had done even a fraction of this damage to a Protected Reserve it would have been treated as a very serious criminal offence. He also made the point that from a practical point of view he and the Inspectorate staff were unaware of the identity of these creatures before the Inquiry commenced and would have had no way of communicating with them.

He confirmed that the Director can authorise a cull of up to twenty percent of any species on a Protected Reserve but in that case the Directorate had to fund that themselves. More than that the Directorate had to apply for a S427 Order but that if that was approved they were entitled to funding from the Treasury.

He stated that strong objections had been received from the Treasury to any such order (so I was right!). They had questioned whether all this effort and expense could be justified for one, arguably insignificant, planet particularly where there was no guarantee of success.

He sympathised with the participants concern at the loss of something as beautiful as Retha and their understandable wish to try to do something but he questioned whether a cull would make any practical difference to the eventual outcome. All the evidence, he said, suggested that the damage already caused was probably irreversible and that this species will almost certainly cause their own destruction whether from disease, pollution, war, accident, famine, or a combination of them all within a very short time span whether or not we do anything.

He did express concern at the continuing legacy of these creatures. Even if they do destroy themselves – the wholesale pollution, radiation, plastic and other waste would remain for thousands of years, possibly for ever. However he concluded that that would be the case whatever we did. He speculated that most of the other species of flora and fauna would eventually recover though, inevitably, some things would be very different from what we remembered.

His depressing conclusion was that a cull of this species would be prohibitively expensive, had no guarantee of success and would take so long to accomplish that it would probably not achieve much. Whilst he agreed Retha had been an amazing place, it was in the scale of things not so significant or important to justify all that expense.

His formal recommendation was that the only practical course was to do nothing and leave this species to destroy themselves by which, he explained, he meant that if they carried on as they were they would inevitably reduce their own population to a fraction of what it currently is. Probably by famine and disease but possibly also war and accidents. He recorded that the collective view of the witnesses was that this would only take between fifty and two hundred years which in our terms is insignificant and that was probably not much longer than most of the suggested remedies would take to implement.

As to Idreji he was scathing about their management of the Reserve and blamed them for what had happened. He made it clear that in his view if they had been doing their job all this would not have happened. He recommended that they be prohibited from running any Protected Reserves in the future.

You could see why Idreji had been objecting.

He ended by recommending that an attempt still be made to contact this species to give them a final opportunity to do something to reduce their population before it was too late, but it was clear he wasn't optimistic.

He also suggested that it would be sensible that the Ranger Team be left in place to monitor the situation and to assist in the eventual reconstruction of the Planet.

I was deeply disappointed. I had desperately hoped we could do something, that Retha could go back to what it had been all that time ago, but, being honest he was right. It was far too late for that, the damage was done. Retha was a lost cause and the best we could do was learn the lessons for the future and move on.

At least Olte should be able to do something to help it recover something of its old beauty even if not the paradise we all remembered.

I had to pass the Retha Base to get to Avsa's hospital so I felt obliged to stop. It had taken less time than I had expected.

As a matter of courtesy Peti notified the Director that I would be coming through. She had told him that he didn't need to be there but obviously he was. He had only just got there so the staff on the base hadn't had any warning. That was probably just as well, otherwise they would have thought they had to make special arrangements.

It was so like the first time. The staff all standing round not sure who I was. The Director making embarrassed attempts to introduce them. The only thing missing was Avsa. Suddenly there he was after all, tall and wonderfully handsome standing at the back just as before. I couldn't help smiling at him but in return I just got a confused and embarrassed look. Eventually the Director took me up to him "This is Warden Olte Signe". I wanted to hug him but it was all a bit public and we just ended up nodding at each other awkwardly.

I think the Director was oblivious to any embarrassment. He suggested I might like to inspect the Base but I just wanted to get off to see Avsa. I asked if Olte could accompany me and we left as soon as was polite.

I should of course have taken that opportunity to personally tell the Director of the Inspector's conclusions, after all it affected him most but I found I just couldn't. The disappointment was still too great. I just wanted to get away.

MESSAGE
From: Warden O Signe
To: Chief Warden A Signe
The Cygnareina has arrived out of the blue. We didn't have any warning. Your message must have worked. You are right she is amazing. Does she know who I am? We are on our way to see you. Make yourself smart. **Olte**

Private Journal

Olte flew next to me. We were nearly there before I realised that he was wearing my Mother's leg ring.

When we got to the hospital he suggested I go in first. As I walked into the little ward Avsa was standing there upright which was difficult in that confined space never designed for species of our size. He looked exactly as I remember him. Tall, rugged and beautiful. Then he turned and I saw the horrible damage to his left side. His wing had been severed half way up. His face was terribly scarred.

I took him in my wings and cried. Partly for him, and partly because all I wanted was to be with him forever. I suppose that's what I always wanted.

We just lay there as close to each other as we could. There seemed no reason to talk.

Finally he said "Have you met our son?"

"Yes he's outside."

After a while we allowed Olte in. They hadn't seen each other since Olte and Prima got him to the hospital all that time ago and they had a lot of catching up to do which allowed me to stand back and enjoy the experience of having a family around me.

Eventually the cramped space got us all down and I suggested that we went outside. Avsa kept saying that he'd be able to fly by himself but obviously he wasn't. Instead I suggested that we should see if we could fly together as we did in the old days.

He put his damaged left wing on top of my right one and we flew off into space. It was uncomfortable at first and I was worried about him but it all came back.

"Where to?"

"Retha".

We flew three abreast across that deep expanse of space. Avsa and I hardly talked. It was enough that we were flying together as we used to.

When we got to Retha we thought about dropping down but I didn't want to take any risks with Avsa. We flew around and around. The longer we flew, the more Avsa's strength returned. Eventually he and I could outfly Olte and he had difficulty keeping up.

It was wonderful. Just like the old days but with our son with us. It would have been even more wonderful if we could have been flying freely over Retha rather than high above.

The rubbish up there was awful and we had to take care. At a distance Retha looked as beautiful as we remembered it and I wanted to leave it that way. We eventually returned to the Retha Base.

Everyone was pleased to see Avsa. Having him around seemed to help to raise their spirits, it probably also helped them get over the embarrassment of me being there.

Olte and the rest of the Ranger Team had to get on with what they were doing so Avsa and I took to going out each day to get away from them. We would go out over Retha. As we became more confident we began to fly just low enough to identify places we had visited all that time ago. We found memories of silly incidents coming back. We were happy. It was like being young lovers again when we had wanted nothing more. This had been our world.

I really didn't want to but eventually I couldn't put things off any longer and there was no choice but to get down and consider my decision. After all that's what I was supposed to be here for.

I reread the Inspector's report. I reluctantly had to agree with all his findings. The Treasury had got what they wanted so there was no reason to hold the Report up any longer. I signed it off and passed it through to the Secretariat so they could notify all the participants. The only problem then was how to tell Avsa and Olte.

I eventually found an excuse to get Olte to come out with us one day. It seemed easier to discuss it flying over Retha.

I explained everything the Inspector said.

"Effectively he's saying it's a lost cause. The Treasury would never agree to the expense."

When I finished Avsa said nothing but he was clearly upset.

"So in the end it just comes down to money?" Olte said. "Isn't there anything you can do?"

"I feel the same. I had hoped that I could do something by taking the Application over and coming here but much as we may hate to admit it he's right. I can't override his recommendations. We all wanted an easy answer but there isn't one."

"Well what are we expected to do?" Olte asked.

I didn't know how to reply. I shared his disappointment but I had had longer to think about it. This had been his home and nothing I was going to say would help. Eventually Avsa broke the silence.

"You've got to stay here" he said to Olte. "You'll be needed to help the planet when these creatures have destroyed themselves. We have no idea whether that will be one single cataclysm or, more likely a combination of them, wars, accident, famine, disease. Whichever it is you must be there to help recover something of the old Retha from this mess".

"So we just wait?" Olte said.

Avsa turned to me "Do we still try to contact them?"

"What's the point" said Olte. "They aren't going to do anything".

"Maybe not. It may just be a waste of time but that's what we are here for" replied Avsa. "Even if it may not have any effect it's our job to at least attempt to get them to realise the damage they are causing. We need to try to get them to begin to understand their responsibilities to their planet. If they really did get on and do something to reduce their population it's just possible they will still have time to reverse things. If not then at least their survivors will know not to make the same mistakes. Your Mother and I will wait here to see what happens. We'll then go and leave you to it."

We eventually returned to Base.

I raised the question of communicating with these humans with Avsa when we next went out.

"How would we do it?" I asked.

"We could post it on their communication system" Avsa suggested.

"Do you know how to?"

"I don't but Hoagfir will".

"Is it alright to ask him?"

"I don't see why not".

We got Hoagfir in when we got back and explained the problem to him He was not someone who was at all overawed at talking to people like me which was actually quite refreshing.

"How would we do it?" I asked.

"I need time to think about it. I'll probably need to talk to Hundil and to Idreji's Department of Communications. Would that be OK?"

I thought about that for a moment. "Yes" I said. "But if you do, it is probably best to make it clear it is official and you are enquiring for the Council".

He returned a while later. "I've got in touch with Hundil and Idreji. Both said they hadn't contacted these creatures. When they knew I was asking for you, Hundil were at pains to make the point that that was not permitted under their charter. I know someone in Idreji's Department of Communications and we had quite a long chat. He was a bit cagey but I got the impression they'd thought about it but hadn't been able to work out how to do it".

"So how do we go about getting the Message to them?" Avsa asked.

"I think the best way might be to try to get one of them to do it for us" Hoagfir said.

"How would we do that?" I asked.

"I was hoping you could help us there".

The power to influence others' thinking is probably the one thing that gave my ancestors our role in the known

Cosmos. It is not one we have used for a very long time, but the Power is still there.

"How would I identify the person?" I asked, "It would have to be just one individual".

"I'll go on to their systems and see if I can find anyone who looks likely" Hoagfir replied.

He came back later. "I have found three. Whether they can do it I don't know but they look hopeful. They all speak English as their main language which is the one we are best at deciphering. They are all probably able to put the Message together and get it out on one of their communication systems".

I tried all three that night. I had difficulty locating the first two. The third was no problem. I went back to Hoagfir.

"Tell me about this one"

"He writes a bit, he's done publishing, he knows about law, he's interested in environmental matters".

"Does he understand our beliefs?"

"I'm not sure but his partner certainly does. She believes all species have an equal right to be here. Even the insect that has just bitten her".

"How do we do it?" Avsa asked.

I had given this some thought. "I think we should simply give him the Inquiry Transcript, that's got everything in it. I suppose it might give it more weight if we could give them the messages between you and Olte as well. Would that be alright?"

"Yes if it helps" he said.

"In that case, he should also have my Private Journal".

We got all those together and I started transmitting them. I could only manage short spells at any one time. It seemed to work better at certain times, possibly when he was asleep. It was harder than I'd expected, particularly communicating in an alien language, and I was finding it a strain. I had been doing it for several days when Olte happened to come in and stood there listening to me. "Can I help?" he said after a while. I looked up surprised. It had never occurred to me that the Power could pass to males. I thought it was only us.

Eventually between the two of us we got it done.

MESSAGE
From: *Director Erigh Jonsen*
To: *Chief Warden A Signe*
Old Friend. *By the time you receive this I will have gone. I cannot believe that I of all people allowed this to happen to you and Retha. If I had done the right things it would never have happened. I am sorry Olte has been left to pick up the pieces. I ask you all to forgive me.* **Erigh**

Private Journal

Avsa showed me the Director's message. It was terribly sad. Why should the life of someone as kind and good as him have been destroyed by one of the very species he had dedicated his life to protecting. I felt guilty that I hadn't talked to him.

I connected with Setar. I told her I wouldn't be coming back. There was a long silence. I suppose it was unfair on her. I had promised her a longer handover period.

"Why" she said.

"Because I want to retire here".

"Isn't this a bit sudden?"

"Yes"

"What have you decided to do about Retha?"

I explained the Inspector's findings "He was right of course but it was desperately disappointing. I hoped there was an answer, that we could return Retha to what it was."

"Was it very beautiful?"

"Yes, it was paradise".

"What have you decided?"

"The Treasury have got their way so there was no reason to hold up the Report any longer. I've signed it off and passed it through to the Secretariat."

"What about Idreji? Did you confirm the Inspector's recommendations?"

"Oh, yes. We mustn't let them get away with this."

"Is there anything else to do?" she asked.

"We will leave the Ranger Team in place to monitor things. We will try to get a message to these creatures in the hope of persuading them to reduce their population whilst they still have time." I explained the Message and how we were transmitting it.

"Would you like to appoint someone there to oversee things when you go? I remember that once, when I was your Mother's Assistant, she created a separate See so there was one person with the authority to take decisions. It would need to be someone who knows the Reserve. Is there anyone suitable?"

"Not really".

"What about the Directorate's Chief Warden. Didn't he used to run the Reserve?"

"Yes but he was very seriously injured and couldn't do it now. Anyway he and I have decided to retire together."

There was a silence and she then asked "What about the current Warden? Would he do?"

"Yes. He is the Chief Warden's son and he was born there but it would probably be best if it wasn't him."

"Why?"

"He's my son".

There was a longer silence this time. Then she came back. "Hadn't you better tell me about them?"

So I told her about Avsa and Olte and Retha.

"I always wondered why you didn't have an heir", she said. "I was never expecting to become Cygnareina, everyone expected you to have a daughter. There was talk that something happened when you were young but no-one really knew. Even though you had a son couldn't you still have had a daughter when you became Cygnareina? Didn't you fulfil the law by giving him away before he was even hatched?"

"It just didn't seem right. I thought we of all beings must lead by example. How can we tell everyone else how many offspring they can have if we do something different ourselves."

"Could Olte do it?"

"Oh yes. He has the Power."

"I never realised it could pass to males! I thought it was only us" she said. "Leave it to me. I'll suggest him. I don't think the Sisters will object. Tell me about him."

"He's gorgeous and wonderful, like his father." Without giving it much thought I went on "You could do a lot worse."

This time she sounded genuinely shocked. But I didn't care. "I don't know if you ever met your father or grandfather but mine weren't much fun. Poor Mother, for all she disapproved of what I did, I think she rather envied me. We've been mating with the same Families for too long. It's time we widened the gene base."

"Is he full Cigne?"

"Oh, yes, but from a very long way back. Avsa obviously isn't from one of the Families but his genes are good. Probably better than yours and mine. He and Olte have fantastic strength and endurance".

She was silent for a while. Then she said "I suppose if I did the Sisters would be happy that I would be having your Grandchild".

I don't know why but that made me overwhelmingly happy. I wouldn't be normal if I didn't like the idea that at least my Grandaughter would be the Cygnareina.

Then as if to change the subject Setar said "What about the human who is passing the Message on. Has he any future role?"

"No, he's just the messenger. All we hope is that he can communicate the Message to as many humans as possible and that they will then do the same."

"How will he get that Message across?" Setar asked.

"We've given him a copy of everything to do with the Inquiry so he can pass it on to his fellow creatures. Everything is in there."

"When will you retire?"

"We don't think it's fair on Olte to leave just yet. We will wait until this species have eventually destroyed themselves. Until then we won't know how many of them will be left and the exact extent of the damage they leave behind. Avsa and I would prefer to be here until then in case Olte needs help. It shouldn't be long – no more than one or two hundred of their years – probably less. We will then have a better idea of what will need to be done to help Retha recover. Can you appoint Olte when we've gone?"

"Yes I'll make sure that happens."

She then asked "Could these creatures do anything to prevent this happening?"

"Oh yes, they could reduce their population very quickly by birth control if they really wanted. It's all in the Report. At the end it's up to them. That's the Message".

THE BEGINNING

MESSAGE

From: Warden Olte Signe

To: HH Cygnara Setar

Your Holiness They left early this morning.

I saw them slowly fade into the distance.

They were so close together it was as if they were one.

Then they were gone.

Olte Signe, Warden, Retha

OFFICIAL NOTICE

With deep sadness the passing
is announced of
Her Supreme Holiness Cygnareina Aretha.

She is succeeded by
Her Holiness Cygnara Setar
who will assume the title of
Her Supreme Holiness Cygnareina Aretha II

S

OFFICIAL NOTICE

I Cygnareina Aretha II, by all the Powers
ordained in me do hereby appoint my beloved
Olte Signe to be Prelate and High Commissioner
of the See of Retha with powers absolute.